"Would you

Omar looked at Stacy ... head.

"Omar?" Stacy prodded with more than a little bit of pleading in her tone.

Omar stopped looking at her. Instead, he kept his focus on the table between them.

"I guess I'm wondering if you're not acting out of impulse, or...desperations," Omar said. Each word was stated with deliberation.

"Do you mind telling me your reservations, Omar?" Stacy asked, before taking a seemingly leisurely sip of water.

"Well, your reasoning seems a little cold. It's as if you think I'm a stud for hire. How long is this to last? Why do I need to be your boyfriend? Will you also publicly dump me when you're done? I do have my pride, you know."

Stacy cringed as he said each statement.

"I'd only need you to help me out for a short bit."

"I'll help under one condition..."

Books by Michelle Monkou

Kimani Romance

Sweet Surrender
Here and Now
Straight to the Heart

Kimani Arabesque

Open Your Heart
Finders Keepers
Give Love
Making Promises
Island Rendezvous

MICHELLE MONKOU

became a world traveler at three years old when she left her birthplace of London, England, and moved to Guyana, South America. She then moved to the United States as a young teen. Being an avid reader, along with her cultural experiences, set the tone for a vivid imagination. It wasn't long before the stories in her head became stories on paper.

In the middle of writing romances, Michelle added a master's of international business to her bachelor's degree in English. Michelle was nominated for the 2003 Emma award for favorite new author. She continues to write romances with complex characters and intricate plots. Visit her Web site for further information, and to sign up for her newsletter and contests, at www.michellemonkou.com.

Having lived on three continents, Michelle currently resides in the Washington, D.C., metropolitan area with her family. To contact her, write to P.O. Box 2904, Laurel, Maryland 20709 or e-mail her at michellemonkou@comcast.net.

Straight to the Heart

MICHELLE MONKOU

KIMANI
ROMANCE

KIMANI PRESS™

ISBN-13: 978-0-373-86034-0
ISBN-10:   0-373-86034-X

STRAIGHT TO THE HEART

www.kimanipress.com

Printed in U.S.A.

Dear Reader,

Welcome once again to the Masterson family, with all their trials and tribulations—and lots of romance. You've met Pierce, Laura and Omar, joining them on their journey to find that special someone. There is still one more sibling, and one more story needed for sister Sheena to find unconditional love.

Will she find it with the man who once captured her heart, or will she have to close a chapter in her life and move on? Only time will tell.

As always, I love to hear from readers. You may contact me at P.O. Box 2904, Laurel, MD 20709 or by e-mail at michellemonkou@comcast.net.

Peace and blessings,

Michelle Monkou
www.michellemonkou.com

To Malcolm and Donsha,
may all your dreams come true.

Chapter 1

Omar Masterson sat back in the chair to mask his unease. The older, stern-faced woman at the end of the conference table held his undivided attention. Not in a good way. What more was there to discuss?

Urban Television Production had taken care of the logistics so that he could proceed smoothly with the documentary here in Montreal, along with getting the appropriate permission from the various third parties. Unless plans had changed, this impromptu meeting face-to-face with barely concealed hostility struck an odd, disquieting note.

"Welcome, Mr. Masterson, I'm Brenda Young, Miss Watts's manager. In a few minutes, you'll meet Josh Briggs and Fred Long, my assistants."

Omar looked over his shoulder for any advance sightings of these men. Their names were delivered like a veiled threat. For now, only Brenda and he sat in the conference room.

"You can call me Ms. Young."

Omar nodded. "And you may call me Omar." He couldn't help adding, "I'm not into formality."

"I called this meeting before you started working to communicate a few rules," Brenda stated.

"I'm sure that UTP has taken care of the necessary details," Omar replied with gentle reassurance. Maybe a touch of his charm could thaw the ice chips hanging off her personality. He certainly wasn't in the position to change or make any deals. "This smells a bit like scripted manipulation."

Brenda shrugged. "Call it protecting assets. I'm a cautious woman who needs extra insurance for peace of mind. This is my final condition for an interview. The studio thought that this would be a good idea." She looked down at her manicured nails, leaving the obvious unsaid, that she hadn't chosen him.

Omar felt skewered by Brenda's gaze.

"That's fantastic and all. However, I expect you

to respect her privacy. Also, you have to run any new ideas outside the preapproved topics past me. Only what I approve will be featured." Brenda adjusted her suit jacket before casting a disdainful look in his direction.

Omar didn't hide his irritation, now that her mind-set was clear. "Brenda, is it?" He emphasized his disregard for her wish for formality. "I don't like having my creative license stifled. I don't take kindly to being addressed like a child."

Brenda punched a button on the telephone. "Josh! Fred! Come in, please." She folded her arms across her ample chest. "I think that we're at the point of our discussion where the nonverbal cues are as important as the verbal."

So the situation had escalated to the gathering of the troops.

"Meet Josh Briggs." Brenda motioned toward a lean, unsmiling, bald man who had an expansive girth that looked rock-solid. "And this is Fred Long." The man stood on her other side. He had a thick neck and beefy hands that matched his entire physique.

Omar figured that though he was new to his job as TV host, his best work occurred when he improvised. Listening to his impulses had never yet proved him wrong. Brenda's mandate had negative consequences for his first major break.

Brenda looked him over.

Omar drew himself up, to quell the nerves. This experience felt like a nerve-racking swim with sharks. Most women came on to him, or at least, depending on their age, thought that he was an adorable young man. This woman was certainly an exception. He'd tag her at being late thirties, early forties. She wore her hair natural, in a close-cropped Afro that topped off her sleek, tailored appearance in a navy-blue pantsuit.

He turned his gaze toward the so-called assistants, with their bodybuilders' physiques, who looked as though they could snap him like a breadstick. Obviously they were amenable to their boss's heavy-handed approach. He guessed he should feel glad that he wasn't meeting them in a dark alley.

Brenda cleared her throat, shifting Omar's attention back to her. "I especially want you to rein in any thought of getting friendly with Stacy while you're on assignment."

"Brenda, gentlemen, I'm a professional. I will treat you and your staff, including Miss Watts, with respect and professionalism. There is no need to come at me as if I'm a hypersexed teen." Omar gritted his teeth, fighting his rising anger.

"Say what you want. You wouldn't be the first to protest with staunch indignation and claim innocence, then try to worm your way into her heart and pocketbook. Just because she helped you land the job with your company, don't read anything into her generosity. Think of it this way. We are her first line of defense. Remember that."

Omar shot out of his seat, pushing back the chair. "You may think I'm a young punk—" Who did these people think they were? He raised his finger, jabbing at the space in front of their faces. "I'm not the one pretending to be wise guys from a bad gangster movie. Don't get it twisted. You all need to check yourselves—"

"Omar!" Stacy burst into the room with a welcoming smile. She crossed the room with light, quick steps and launched herself into his arms. "I couldn't believe it when I heard that you would be doing the interview." She hugged him again. "How lucky am I?"

Omar put on a small smile for her sake. The matter at hand, however, was far from over.

Stacy's exuberance managed to evaporate the bad vibes. Her upbeat entry hit the atmosphere like sunlight burning through a dense fog. He'd always thought that she could be Angela Bassett's daughter: the color of golden-brown sugar, high cheekbones and eyes with a slant that revealed Native American heritage somewhere along the family tree. What he liked most was her sculpted lips, full and wide, that had a distinct shape, lifting at the ends as if she perpetually smiled.

While Stacy repeatedly hugged him between bursts of chatter, he looked over at Brenda and her two sitting bulls. Their collective disapproval hadn't waned a bit. He was sure that there would be cause for another meeting. The next time, he'd be the one calling the shots.

"Are we all set? I want to steal Omar away so we can catch up before we have to get down to business." Stacy looked at Omar and then her management team.

Omar nodded. "We can get started with the interview tomorrow."

"Great. Then let's go have some fun," Stacy urged, with a wide grin that could rival a teeth-whitening advertisement.

"I'd love to," Omar stated, arching his eyebrows at Brenda. He already classified the threesome as an odd partnership. Hopefully Stacy would share specific information that could reveal why he had become enemy number one.

Omar followed Stacy out of the room, glad to be free of present company. They moved through the building, dodging the crew busy with set changes. For a few minutes, Omar studied the goings-on. Life on a movie set seemed far busier than he'd imagined. A few of the principles he recognized from entertainment news. He had to admit that his nerves were on edge as he thought about his job and the close proximity he'd been in with major and minor celebrities. Did he have what it would take to be an interviewer of the stars? Women dominated the industry, but he wanted his fighting chance.

"Hey, don't get quiet on me." Stacy nudged him.

"Taking it all in." Omar playfully returned her nudge.

She hooked her arm in his, and together they strolled out into the crisp Canadian air. A series of trailers and RVs sat parked on the perimeter of the set. Stacy led him to an impressive, sleek RV that shouted *big money,* with the latest high-tech gadgetry.

"Let's get out of this cold." Stacy pulled the door closed behind him. She blew on her hands, vigorously rubbing them together. "Want some coffee?"

"Sounds great." Omar waited a few minutes before removing his jacket.

Montreal's weather surprised him; September seemed a bit early for temperatures in the low sixties. The sticky warmth of Atlanta's late-summer temperature had skewed his clothing choice. He wore a thin windbreaker, short-sleeved shirt and lightweight slacks. He'd been clenching his teeth to keep from shivering. His face still stung from the stiff breeze. Maybe after a cup of hot coffee the feeling in his exposed body parts could return to normal.

Stacy's conversation hadn't let up, which was fine with him. Her upbeat voice and sincere intent offered the welcome that he'd anticipated. Meeting her again was everything that he'd hoped it would be.

He nodded and appropriately grunted as Stacy's conversation ranged from the weather to her busy schedule during and after the movie. He was glad that, although briefly, he'd have Stacy all to himself. Maybe they could have a casual friendship, nothing more.

His sister, Sheena, scolded him for running through his women like the bulls running in Pamplona. Though there was more than a grain of truth in the ridiculous analogy, he had no intention of making Stacy a conquest. After all, she was a woman living the uptown life. What could he offer?

Stacy poured the coffee and prepared it to his instructions. "Let's catch up. I've been babbling for the past fifteen minutes. What's going on with you? Is the job still fun?"

Omar took his mug. "The job is everything I thought it would be. Each day is a new experience. I'm still learning and when I think that I've finally got it, there's something new to learn. And the people I've met. Wow! Their names read like a who's who on today's artists. Some are nice and live up to their image. Others need a quick course on professional etiquette."

"Sounds like this job has stretched you beyond your wildest dreams." Stacy raised her mug in a salute. Her gaze openly admired him, which only slightly embarrassed him.

Everything about this woman tempted him. In these close quarters, even her perfume had the power to give Brenda's prediction some credence. Restraint was key. Otherwise, one week could feel like one year.

Stacy sat opposite him, blowing at her coffee. Darn, it would be tough to stick with his action plan. The way she formed her lips to blow offered a natural pucker.

Omar waited for her to say more. Their conversation had dwindled into contemplative silence.

"Sorry. Lots of things going on in my mind," Stacy offered.

"Don't apologize," Omar replied. "I'm the one who should apologize for keeping you from your work. I came to introduce myself, get acquainted with the environment and finalize some of the logistical details for tomorrow. I've kept you from your work long enough." He set down his cup and stood.

"Please don't leave." Stacy approached and placed a restraining hand on his arm. "I really haven't made friends on the set and I look forward to chatting with a familiar soul." She made a face. Her coaxing smile played with his emotions.

Omar nodded, covering her hand with his. He knew all too well what it felt like to be on the outside with no one taking him seriously. A few more minutes in her company wouldn't hurt anything.

A loud knock startled both of them, interrupting further conversation.

Stacy opened the RV door. Omar couldn't see the visitor, but noted from the sound of the voice that the person was a man. He strained to hear, but only heard the deep rumble of the man's muted voice. Stacy followed suit with hushed responses. Then whatever the man said drew her anger in a raised tone. She looked over her shoulder and mouthed an apology to him, before facing the mysterious visitor.

"I'll be there in a second," she said in a tight voice. "Marty should be contacted."

"He's already on the phone." The man matched her raised voice.

"Good. Tell everyone I'll be there." Stacy snapped the door closed, but remained facing it. Her head drooped. With a visibly shaky hand, she smoothed the hair from her face.

Omar didn't wait any further to read the situation. Instead he walked up behind her and lightly placed his hands on her shoulders. Her small frame tensed. He searched his mind to find the right thing to say. She obviously was very upset.

"Can I help?" Omar asked, not sure what he was volunteering for, but hating to see her so distressed.

She shook her head.

"Then I'll get out of your hair." He understood why she wouldn't confide in him. He pulled out one of his business cards and searched his jacket pockets for a pen. "Call me on my cell if you need to talk."

"Can you wait here until I return?"

Her plea touched him.

Omar nodded. He might not be able to solve her problem, but he could offer a comforting friendship.

"Good."

Before he could ask any questions, she exited the RV and he watched her head back to the building. Omar waited until she disappeared into the adjacent office before closing the door. This trip so far, with its various nuances, created a zigzag path leading to the unknown. Without much encouragement, he'd volunteered to step onto the path.

Maybe he could blame his excitement on seeing Stacy again. Maybe his desire to impress her with his new job was at fault.

Or could he be motivated by no more than how fantastic she looked, and how his body reacted whenever she brushed past him?

While he waited, he called his office to check in. As he filled in his boss, he casually surveyed the area. There were a few framed photographs of Stacy decorating the RV. But a majority of the photos were of a little girl and an older boy. Their resemblance was so uncanny that Omar suspected they were siblings. He hadn't heard of Stacy having children, unless she'd been a young teen when she'd had them. Maybe they were her niece and nephew. Whoever they were, the two certainly had a pictorial history in her RV from infancy to the present.

Another group of photos caught his attention. He ended his call for the opportunity to examine them more closely. Each photo was of Stacy and a different man. Each man sported heavy bling jewelry. Some smiled, displaying more glitter on their teeth. A few were dressed in designer suits, wearing shades, looking slick and dangerous all at the same time. He recognized a few of the men from the hip-hop world. The way Stacy smiled and pressed her body against these men made him wonder.

"Is this my competition?" he muttered.

Stacy sat at the table beating back the nausea. This phone call had tied her stomach in knots.

Brenda was running the conference call with her lawyer, Marty. As Brenda shared the details of the latest disturbing call, Stacy refused to accept that everything she'd worked for in this short time could be threatened by one man. She listened to Brenda retell the latest threat to blow up her reputation with so much mudslinging that her career would be automatically in the toilet. She hadn't been around long enough to build a legacy to counteract seedy claims. But the situation angered her. Climbing to the top was no accident.

Josh and Fred made quite the frightening pair as her bodyguards, unsmiling and furious. She was tempted to give them the approving nod to make mincemeat of her tormentor. Instead, she leaned forward and cleared her throat. "Marty, do you think this guy is serious? That he'll take it all the way?"

"Yes. What you don't know and I recently learned is that he's scheduled a press conference for next week. I called his lawyers and they said you must pay him to keep his mouth shut."

"What!" Stacy exploded from the chair. She looked at Brenda, hoping that she had an instant solution to this crazy mess. "Pay him? Never!" What had gotten into Antonio's head? But she didn't need anyone to answer that question for her. Antonio Perez, her former boyfriend and manager, hadn't taken her departure from his personal and professional life very well. He was never without female company and didn't bother to be discreet. On the professional front he had controlled her career like an overseer. She blamed her youth and naiveté for ever giving him control of her career, even after they'd broken up.

"I wouldn't advise paying him," Marty said. "Brenda can provide a noncommittal response, while we work on the legal angle."

"I don't think he cares about the law. This is personal," Stacy countered. "He expects me to come crawling to him."

"He wants back in," Brenda said. "Have you had any contact with him recently?"

Stacy shook her head.

"Did you mention him in any interviews?" Marty questioned.

"No." Stacy searched her memory for any clue. She had left Antonio and her neighborhood a month after her twenty-first birthday. He'd made a last-ditch effort to get her back, furious that Brenda was also sending her to a "finishing school" to polish her for the very public life of a celebrity.

"What's the worst he could say about you?" Marty asked.

Stacy opened her mouth to give her opinion, but embarrassment stopped her.

Brenda touched her hand. "Marty, let's just say that he could add a layer of unpleasantness with his own colorful rendition of her past."

"That's why I should talk to the media." Stacy didn't want Antonio giving his two cents on her tough childhood—her being raised by a mother with substance-abuse issues. Then she had moved to an aunt who had meant well, but hadn't had the emotional capacity to take care of a young child. The journey had continued with child protective services, which had led to a foster home before she'd reconnected with cousins.

Brenda looked doubtful. Marty didn't respond, either.

"There's nothing to think about. We need to beat the timing of his press conference and kill his thunder," Stacy prompted.

"Stacy, give me an hour. I'm not comfortable with that approach," Marty said. "I'll call you back." The call ended.

"We never lied about your background," Brenda reminded her.

"It's more than that. Some details we didn't share. The court of public opinion could cast me aside, and then I'd be a liability. Will I get offers from studios? Will I become the spokeswoman for certain products?" Stacy didn't like feeling defensive or sounding paranoid.

Fred snapped his fingers. "What if we matched her up?"

Her manager leaned forward, her eyes gleaming.

"Match me up with whom?" Stacy couldn't believe that this was the solution.

"Look, celebs are always linked to the latest star and it's not always coincidence. Remember that faded movie star and the young gangster rapper? Gives the perception that you're in the *in* crowd and gets the younger fans on your side. They have the economic weight to make it happen."

"Yeah, but that relationship ended ugly in the media. And frankly, I'm not tying myself to any man who wears a grill on his teeth and a do-rag on his head. Certain things should stay on stage and not become a part of the daily wear."

Stacy eyed Brenda as she headed toward the window. She had not voiced an opinion. Even Fred waited for Brenda's response.

"This is a classy city." Brenda pointed toward the partially obstructed view of the city. "Tourists can admire the impressive architecture that created this city around the four nations that called it home."

Stacy nodded, thinking that this wasn't the time for a pro-Montreal moment.

Stacy got up and walked over to stand beside Brenda. They watched the people bustle to and fro. She saw the diversity, a melting pot of original colonists, consisting of the Irish, English, French and Scots with millions of newer arrivals from Africa, the West Indies, Italy and even America.

"Montreal is a piece of Europe on this side of the continent. Don't you agree?" Brenda asked with an appreciative smile. "When we began our partnership, we had goals to reach the top. But you've got to admit, kiddo, that standing in Montreal on a film set two and half years later beats our timeline." Brenda took a deep breath and turned to face her.

And then Stacy understood Brenda's point.

If she didn't play her next move correctly, all of this could be plucked out of her grasp. The movie producers were bound to fire her for the negative publicity. After all, she wasn't the star of the movie, and Brenda had done fast talking and called in a few favors to get a hip-hop personality on the roster. Maybe Fred wasn't so far off the mark.

"I'm liking what I'm hearing from you, Fred. Let me make a few calls." Brenda snapped up her cell phone earpiece and set her date planner on the table in front of her.

"I'll be right back." Stacy would rather not hear Brenda begging on her behalf. She exited the room. Where was a chapel when you needed one?

Maybe a good, fortifying prayer could counteract Antonio's dirty fight ahead. Suddenly she remembered that she'd asked Omar to stick around. How was she going to face him? He'd know something was wrong. She tried to get herself together before entering the RV. Her mood lightened when she saw Omar still sipping coffee, writing on a notepad. The scene soothed her a bit. She softly closed the door, respecting that he was at work. He looked up and offered a welcoming smile. He instantly made her feel safe. Plus he was certainly a treat to the eyes. Tall, slim, *GQ* model features, with a sexy, confident smile that reduced her to a babbling mess.

Fred's suggestion again intruded. Maybe he had something. Stacy took a deep breath. A smidgen of excitement simmered. There really was no time to debate the pros and cons.

"I need to talk to you and my management team. Got a couple more minutes to spare?"

"Uh-oh, doesn't sound good. Could I get a hint?" Omar shut his writing pad and sat back.

"I'm mulling around a couple of career ideas." Stacy tried to keep her tone even to ease the tension that immediately dictated Omar's body language.

"And you need to discuss this with me?"

"And my management team," Stacy elaborated.

Omar frowned. "Do they know that you're bringing me into your discussion?"

"Hey, it's not a big deal. I just want to throw out an idea that I think you might be interested in. You can say no, okay?" Stacy laughed, hoping that Omar would relax. If he was this nervous, there was no way that he would consider her strange plan. She fought the urge to sink on the couch, grab a fat chocolate bar and eat her way through the remainder of the afternoon.

"You look like you lost your best friend." Omar approached her. "Don't mean to sound difficult. I've been through so many discussions with the production team, and then your management team, that I don't know whether I'm coming or going." He rubbed his forehead, emitting an apologetic chuckle. "After you." He motioned toward the door.

Stacy led the way back to the conference room. Omar didn't deserve to be dragged into her mess. This only proved to her how empty her life was that she could consider an outrageous solution with someone who was practically a stranger.

Brenda, Fred and Josh hadn't moved out of their huddle, although additional empty water bottles littered the conference table.

Brenda looked up at their entrance. "No luck so far, kiddo. But I'm not done."

"No luck with what?" Stacy shrugged, not wanting to deal with any other ideas before she had a chance to talk.

"Why is he here?" Brenda looked at Omar with a disagreeable frown.

"I asked him to join us." Stacy looked at Brenda, wondering why her disapproval came so quickly at the sight of Omar. "Is that a problem?" She noted that Omar matched Brenda's reaction with an equal look of distaste.

"I don't think it is appropriate to bring in outsiders."

Stacy flinched at the cold dismissal. The last thing she needed was for Omar to walk away from this obvious disrespect. Right now, she needed something from him. This wasn't going to be an easy sell to either party. She took a seat at the head of the table and poured herself a glass of water, hoping that no one saw her hand shake.

"Omar, please have a seat. Brenda, Fred and Josh, I'll need you to take a back seat and let me do the driving." Stacy decided to treat this meeting like one of her singing performances, where she had to add a dose of street flavor to her lyrics to get across her message.

Silence dropped like a heavy boulder on the room. Everyone froze. Now that she had their attention, Stacy rose to take center stage. Her sense of ownership, leadership and survival kicked in. She had to get everyone united around her proposal.

Her watch showed that fifteen minutes remained before Marty called. A solution had to be in place. She looked at Omar, hoping that he wouldn't think too badly of her. Under different circumstances, she would have liked to explore a friendship, or even something more, with him. But after her bold request, there would be no guarantee.

"Omar, I'm being blackmailed by a former boyfriend and manager. In a matter of hours, he plans to open the doors to my life. It's a history that doesn't play well in the media. Without enough time to come up with a perfect solution, I must ask you for a very big favor."

"Yes?" Omar prodded. His curious gaze fastened on her face.

"No!" Brenda exploded.

"Would you be my boyfriend?"

Stacy now understood what "crackling tension in the air" meant.

"How is that helping the situation?" Brenda looked at Stacy as if she had grown an extra head.

Stacy didn't want to respond. "Omar?" she prodded with more than a little bit of pleading in her tone.

"You can't seriously consider this man," Brenda continued. "You know nothing about him. You need someone with proven credentials, with a healthy reputation. For heaven's sake, you need someone with class or you'll be making another mistake with another man."

Brenda's disgust grated on Stacy's nerve. Not only had she insulted Omar, but her manager also slammed her. Omar didn't look at her, as she tried to offer a silent apology. Instead, he focused on the table with his hands steepled against his chest.

He finally responded, each word stated with deliberation. "Not that I agree with your management team's overzealous nature to see only the worst in a young brother, but I'm wondering if you're not acting out of impulse or desperation. Believe me, I understand having to feel that way, which can cause you to leap into a more difficult position."

Why was everyone treating her as if she were a child? Not too long ago, Brenda had been on the phone trying to find a boyfriend for hire. When she'd met Omar back in Atlanta a year ago, she'd sensed that they were mutually attracted. Then she'd thought that she was being foolish and it was only her imagination. Besides, she had just started in her career and put any ideas of a relationship with anyone at the bottom of her priorities.

"Do you mind telling me what your reservations are, Omar?" she asked before taking a seemingly leisurely sip of water.

He gestured to no one in particular around the room. "Your reasoning seems a little cold. Like I'm for hire. How long is this to last? Why do I need to be your boyfriend? Will you also publicly dump me when you're done? I do have my pride, you know."

Brenda snorted. "Let me be the sole voice of common sense."

Stacy nodded, although she really didn't want to hear what Brenda had to say. Her own conscience roared its disapproval with disgusting logic.

"Homeboy over here is still a newbie in his TV-host spot. I'm not sure he understands what it would mean to be the temporary boyfriend of a rising star. I only have to look in his eyes and see that he's a restless soul with no solid foundation— a process that comes with maturity. At my age and in this business, I've seen a lot. Personally I don't think he's good enough to be connected with your image. No offense. We worked too hard to take unnecessary risks. Stacy, give me the remainder of the day and I'll get someone for you. Someone who knows the rules of the entertainment game. No one that we would have to watch over to make sure he doesn't take advantage of you or your money."

Stacy cringed at each statement. Coming from the street, she'd suffered similar narrow-minded thinking and actual insults. She understood how words could be used like weapons to cut and slash away at a fragile ego. Granted, nothing about Omar could be mistaken as fragile, but he didn't deserve this.

Omar let Stacy play peacemaker. Her actions gave him time to ratchet down his anger. Why did this woman hate him? As much as he flicked off her comments, some of her words hit their mark. He'd shifted jobs and residences in a short period of time, constantly seeking, reevaluating, discovering. But the one thing that she indicted him for with no evidence was being a cheat. That accusation burned him. This woman in her fashion-designer finery, show-business crassness and distrusting nature dared to call him a leech.

"Omar has been nothing but honorable," Stacy continued, still defending him.

He'd admit that he had thought about Stacy long before he came on this assignment. From the first day he'd met her, he'd recognized a spirit surrounding her that drew him in. Her public persona did impress him, but he didn't perceive that as being superficial. He understood that she had to commit to hard work and discipline to land on the path of success. How many times had his big brother, Pierce, said those very words to him?

"Omar? Is this right? Are you honorable? From where I sit, I'd suspect that you're a chisel-faced heartbreaker. Guys your age are nothing but stone-cold players. My job is to protect Stacy from the likes of you. Unlike her, I'm immune to your charm."

Omar acknowledged a suspicious glint in Brenda's eyes with a curt nod. She wasn't the only one who could read someone. Here was a woman who spoke not only from a business sense, but from personal misfortune. If he stayed his ground, he could call her out on the latter and make an enemy for life. Or he could be strategic in a way that might not elicit her support, but still earn a grudging acceptance for his part in this crazy scenario.

Omar finally looked at Stacy, who nervously worked her hands. "Stacy, I'd have preferred that you ask me privately to consider this."

"Honestly, I didn't think that there would be this much discussion. I'd only need you to help me out for a short bit."

"I'll help under one condition."

"See, I rest my case." Brenda slammed down her fist.

Omar ignored the manager. Her outrage motivated him to make his next move.

"I want to talk to you alone." Deliberately he raised his eyes from Stacy's gaze to meet Brenda's glare.

"Brenda, guys, excuse us," Stacy prompted.

Brenda didn't move. But neither did Omar. Maybe he was flexing his muscle. But Brenda had brought the fight squarely to his feet.

"If you're going to stay in the room, then I'll go find an empty room." Stacy led the way to the door.

"Fine. We'll leave." Brenda threw up her hands. "Do me a favor? Don't agree to anything he says without discussing it with me."

Stacy didn't answer, her attention focused on Omar. He waited until the others exited the room. He still didn't know exactly what he wanted.

"I will help you in any way that I can," Omar began.

"Great. I know you're worried about being paid. That's not a problem," Stacy rushed.

"I don't want money," Omar replied, hurt that she had automatically assumed that he was focused on money. "I want to do this because I genuinely like you."

"I like you, too, Omar. It's one of the reasons that I'm comfortable approaching you with this plan. And I really won't need you for a long time. You're here for a week, right?"

"Four days, but I could probably stretch it. But I'm game to give this a whirl as long as we last. And I'm hoping that's for a long time."

"Oh, but it won't be for long," Stacy replied.

"Ouch." Maybe he was losing his touch. He didn't know what more he had to say to let her know of his interest.

"What did I say?" Stacy's smile drooped.

"Why should we only make this a temporary thing? I'm interested in you, getting to know you. Why don't we make good use of the time and situation?"

"Omar, I can't possibly think of a relationship, especially when I have an ex-boyfriend ready to wreak havoc with my life."

"Will I have to accompany you to public events?" Stacy nodded.

"Will you be acknowledging me in interviews?"

"Yep."

"Then what's wrong with us sharing a drink in the evenings, enjoying a chat on the phone? I'm not taking your money because this means more to me than a business transaction." He sighed. "I guess in normal circumstances within your circle, I wouldn't be your top pick."

Stacy shook her head, not looking at him. He desperately wanted to read her eyes, but she focused on the top button of his polo shirt.

"Is it because of what Brenda said?" He stepped forward, closing the distance between them. He raised her chin with a crook of his finger. Stubbornly she kept her eyes lowered. "Look at me, Stacy." Her eyes locked with his. He leaned forward slightly, afraid that she'd withdraw in alarm. Her only reaction was to open her eyes wider. He stepped into her personal space, so close that he felt the warmth of her breath against his lips. "I'm not touting an image," he said softly.

"No. But I think that you have a touch of the bad boy in you."

"Does that hurt my chances?" He touched her cheek and lowered his face, keeping his lips a mere breath away from hers. Her nostrils flared, her eyes closed and a sweet, cinnamon-scented sigh escaped in a whispery puff of air. He kissed her in a tight embrace. Acting on impulse did bring out his best work. His passion matched hers in a heated response of lips meeting, tongues intertwined, arms locked.

There was no turning back. He'd fallen hard from a dizzying height, free-falling with utter satisfaction, making him not want to land on firm ground.

"Stacy, do you need me in here?"

Brenda's ill-timed interruption ruptured the seal of their kiss and tight embrace, snapping them apart like a taut rubber band.

Chapter 2

"I do not believe what I'm seeing." Brenda stormed into the room.

Stacy froze. Her mind shouted the appropriate expletive. Being caught by Brenda matched the trauma of her many trips to the principal's office. This devilish man had kissed her, sending her mind into a spin. And not a soft peck, but a kiss that electrified her entire body like a race car shooting around a track in a blaze of combustible heat.

Omar took a step forward, blocking Stacy from Brenda's wrath. She admired his actions. From the erect position of his shoulders, she suspected that, unlike her, he held no regrets. Great for him that he could remain calm. Her pulse hadn't returned to normal. In an effort to stem Brenda's tirade, which was certain to come and to last for a lengthy duration, Stacy took a deep breath and stepped out to stand at his side.

"Stacy, since this man can't open his mouth to provide a satisfactory explanation, then maybe you can tell me what is going on in here. Gosh, I could choke you."

"Brenda, calm down. This isn't Omar's fault. I'm an adult, although you still like to talk to me as if I'm a young child." Stacy's cheeks grew steadily hotter.

"I couldn't help myself," Omar offered with a shrug. "She's beautiful. I think that spontaneous kissing will make our relationship look more genuine to the public, at least from my point of view." Omar added the last part with a huge grin.

The phone rang. Stacy breathed easier, happy for the reprieve. Her mouth still tingled from the sensual memory. No doubt that chemistry existed between Omar and her. The one thing she knew for sure was that running her fingers along Omar's neck with her body pressed against the entire length of his stirred a longing in her. Electrical pulses ignited a sensual awakening.

"It's the lawyer. Could you get everyone back in the room?" Brenda kept her angry glare as she resumed her stiff business persona.

"Marty, we can move ahead with our plans. Stacy has hired someone to pretend to be her love interest for the short duration," Brenda stated drily.

Stacy squirmed. Brenda couldn't have done a better job of reinforcing Omar's role-playing. However, if she got wind of Omar's change of plans, they'd still be in a raging debate. Hopefully Omar would let it be and would not hold on to his position stubbornly.

"Good. Who's the lucky person?" the lawyer asked.

"Omar Masterson." Brenda didn't elaborate. Her mouth curled in a frown.

"He understands what is expected of him?" Marty inquired.

Brenda arched her penciled brows. "Yes. I'm sure he understands where we're coming from. By the way, he's also the one who'll interview Stacy, so this is a good opportunity to use his resources."

Omar cleared his throat. "This is Omar. Glad to be of service. I'm sure my network will be surprised, but I'll deal with my end of things."

"Okay, Omar, have your people call me if there are any issues. In the meantime, can you provide the final version of your first interview? I've also

got to get with the movie producers because we
had an agreement that there would be no information about the movie until the studios started their
publicity machine. Well, let's go do our things
and put a stop to Antonio."

"Thanks, Marty," Stacy said, truly grateful for
her lawyer's calm, reasonable input. Too bad he
couldn't be here in person. Tension crackled in the
room, hinting at an impending explosion. She had
no doubt that a new fight would break out between
Brenda and Omar.

Sure enough, after the call ended, Brenda
turned toward them with her arms folded against
her chest, her face fixed for a battle. But Stacy
wasn't in the mood. Plus she was a big girl.
Brenda needed to stop treating her as if she didn't
have good sense.

And Omar needed to wipe off his smug smirk.
She couldn't deal with their skirmishes. Just
because he had delivered a knee-buckling kiss
didn't mean that she was willing to give in to his
crazy proposal. At least the one ray of light was
that he could serve as a diversion to her frustra-
tions.

"I've been in the business long enough to see
stars crash and burn by the company that they keep.
Then they look back at their life and wonder why
they didn't see the wreck coming," Brenda said.

"I respect your experience, Brenda. But you don't have to worry about Omar taking advantage of me. We're going to do this, get it over with and then Omar will go on to his next project." Stacy walked to the door, letting both of them know that any further discussion was over. "Omar, when you've talked to your folks about the latest development, give me a buzz to tell me how it went. I'm filming a scene tonight at eight and I don't know how late the session will be."

Stacy retired alone to her RV. The day had worn her out. It didn't make sense to head to her hotel. Her mobile home served as a retreat from the hectic pace, the interior decorated with mementos to stave off homesickness. Lavender-scented candles decorated a path from the small sitting area through the dinette area to her sleeping quarters. Small framed photographs of her niece and nephew served as reminders that there was such a thing as a normal, happy childhood. As an added touch, she traveled with her assorted stuffed zoo animals that now took residence on her bed.

A huge yawn overtook her. She was more tired than she'd thought. A nice long shower appealed to her before diving into bed and she took one with no dillydallying. Dressed in sweats, she gratefully sank into bed. The TV played, her ritual for falling asleep.

Darkness didn't agree with her too much; it

was a time of day when her world as a teen had grown scarier and unpredictable.

The few gigs she'd got had kept her out late. If she wasn't dodging the drug dealers and the addicts, she had to avoid lecherous, much older men who couldn't take no for an answer.

A gang would have offered protection. She was never part of one, but was astute enough to know that she had to stay on the gangs' good sides while she lived in the neighborhood. Crime had never attracted her—too stressful, what with cops performing raids on certain neighborhoods. Her family structure might have been downright shady, but she still had enough dignity and self-respect to avoid that slippery, hellish slope. Living in a juvenile home which had an assortment of the innocent and the not-so-innocent, Stacy didn't need tough love from a loved one to keep her straight.

Skirting the seedy side of life threatened her plans to be a strong, classy, independent woman. Only Antonio had known her one big secret. No one, not Brenda and certainly not Omar, could know, until the time was right. Omar would be in her life for a short period, but she cared about his opinion. A few stolen moments in his arms made her feel normal and desirable.

What a fantasy, she thought, as she drifted to sleep.

* * *

After the meeting, Omar checked in to his hotel. He'd planned on meeting Stacy and her team and then heading to the hotel before checking out the nightlife. In a scenario that fitted a TV sitcom, he had been insulted by Brenda, intimidated by the brawny assistants and roped into Stacy's potential scandal. Well, maybe he wasn't such a reluctant participant. Playing Stacy's boyfriend wasn't far from his wishful thinking.

A quick taxicab ride brought him to the grand Royal Canada Montreal Hotel. The impressive building seemed to be lifted from the streets of Paris. UTP's selection of a luxury hotel surprised Omar. Such amenities for him with his short tenure with the company shocked him. Maybe the secretary hadn't realized the type of hotel when she scheduled the reservations. He grinned. There would be no complaint from him. Thankfully, his check-in process moved quickly. Within minutes, his footsteps echoed against the marbled floor. He looked forward to seeing his room, or suite, as the hotel clerk referred to it.

The king-sized bed with crisp white linen called for his travel-weary body. No argument came from him. He threw himself back, groaning as his sore muscles protested before surrendering to complete relaxation. He couldn't move if he wanted to. He'd wait until tomorrow before calling his boss with the latest development. Besides, he wasn't sure what if anything he would tell.

Admiring the stylish, ornately carved furniture and ceramic decorative accents, he enjoyed the illusion of a VIP. A brochure sat propped against the pillow, obviously for his attention. The tri-folded stationery on linen cardstock boasted the hotel's hundredth anniversary. What scandals and romances had occurred in the posh surroundings over the century?

He didn't care for any personal sticky situations. But he wouldn't be averse to a little romantic fling. In his lavish digs for the next few days, he could go along with the illusion that he was the perfect match for Stacy.

Too bad he didn't have anyone to call and brag to. A string of ex-girlfriends wasn't an option. He was too much of a loner to have bonded with the guys on the job.

His older brother, Pierce, would have liked such a call. As head of their family, he would use the situation to lecture him about living over his head or living off other people's successes.

His older sister, Sheena, would listen. She was a similar thinker without the condescending attitude. This elaborate plan wouldn't impress her. Her mind-set would question the disadvantages. There weren't too many of his schemes or girlfriends that she approved of.

He picked up the phone at his bedside. His other sister, Laura, was a kindred spirit. She'd become more fun and easy-spirited now that she'd fallen madly in love with a professional track athlete. Her romantic outlook made her the perfect confidant. He dialed her number.

The phone rang. He looked at the clock to determine what her schedule might be. As a physical therapist, Laura had set hours. But if there were any special circumstances—a sporting event or late practice—she changed her scheduled routine. At the fifth ring, just as he decided not to leave a message and simply hang up, his sister answered breathlessly, "Hello?"

"Laura? Did I catch you at a bad time?"

"No. I've been out gardening all day. I'm off for a couple of days to finish up my landscaping project."

"What? Is this what happens after you get married?" Omar teased.

Laura chuckled. "You're too young to know."

"Maybe. Maybe not."

"Okay, what news are you trying to tell me? Wait, am I the first one you called?"

Laura's excitement brought a smile to his face. "Yes, you're the only one I've called. But I'm not making any grand announcements."

"I don't believe you. I'll play along, though. Where the heck are you?"

"Montreal. Remember the TV-hosting job?"

"You mean they haven't fired you? My brother who has never held a job for more than six months is now a steady working professional. This *is* big news," Laura teased.

"Pierce would be proud to know that I'm coming into my own." His brother's approval meant a lot to him.

"Listen, Pierce has his own family now. Despite his power trips, he means well. After all, he was the one left in charge of us. We couldn't have been an easy responsibility."

"Oh, goodness, now you're sounding like a softie." Listening to his sister defend Pierce made him realize how much they all had grown and gone off in different directions. A large part of their individual successes lay at Pierce's feet, yet, when he was younger, Omar couldn't give Pierce the respect that he deserved. With this job and what he wanted to accomplish, he hoped to prove to Pierce that he'd been worth any sacrifices.

"There's another family update. I think that

Sheena is still having problems with Carlton. Things aren't looking good. I hate seeing her so unhappy."

"It's hard to believe this is happening when they have been married for so long and have survived so many challenges." Omar recalled how their family had almost fractured when their father had left. His older sister would hate to relive that experience by having her own child suffer. As a result of their family struggles, the Mastersons were a strong unit. His immediate impulse was to pack his bags and head home to be there for Sheena.

"I've talked to her. She's hanging in there. Sheena and our sister-in-law, Haley, have bonded. Can you believe that? Haley has been a good friend for her, considering her own experiences. Tread lightly when you speak to Sheena. She does like her privacy."

Omar accepted what Laura said. He wasn't sure if marriage would ever be a choice for him. His faith in the institution had been formed by his parents' faulty history.

"Hey, you called me," Laura prompted. "What else is happening?"

"Well, I wanted to let you know that I'm dating someone. Don't know how hip you are, but I'm dating Stacy Watts."

"Stacy Watts! Of course I know her. Well, I

mean, I've heard of her. Remember, I work with college kids. How the heck did you manage that?"

"Thanks for that show of confidence. I'm here to interview her, but I'd met her in Atlanta, remember?"

"Oh yeah. She was pretty low-key. Why the heck is she interested in you?"

Omar heard the teasing, but also Laura's frank assessment of the situation. "She likes me. I like her. Isn't that how things get started?" He didn't hide his irritation.

"I'm concerned for her sake since you do have a habit of going through women. Do you want me to do a roll call?"

"No. Maybe I've matured. Give me some credit. She's a wonderful woman who is striking out on her own path. I admire that."

"I bet that's not all you admire."

"Would it help if I bring her to meet you?" Omar didn't have a clue how he was going to manage that one.

"Yes!"

The sharp, familiar ring of the phone jarred Stacy awake. The room had darkened considerably. She closed her eyes, wishing for the comfort of sleep to reclaim its hold. But the caller wasn't having it. She blindly reached for the offending object.

"Hello," she growled, her throat thick from sleep.

"Sounds as if I woke you," a familiar voice teased.

"Guess I was exhausted." Omar's sexy voice pried open her eyelids and nudged her body fully awake.

"I've got a cup of delicious hot dark chocolate with a dollop of whipped cream for you."

He played dirty. Not bad. Anything chocolate could get her to reveal trade secrets. "Where are you?" Her mouth anticipated the rich, bold flavors.

"Sitting in the cold outside your RV."

Stacy sprang out of bed as if he were standing at the foot of her bed. Her hands immediately smoothed her wrinkled sweats. Halfway down the hallway, she tested her breath, then made a quick detour to the bathroom.

Her delay to answer the door resulted in Omar belting away on a John Legend ballad. He didn't sound bad at all. She paused behind her front door, enjoying his rendition of the singer's latest popular tune. His lighthearted attitude was contagious, and soon she joined him by humming the tune.

"You know it's cold out here!" Omar shouted.

Stacy promptly opened the door, giggling at his over-the-top behavior. First, she relieved him of the hot beverage and took a sip, then she stepped aside and motioned him in. "You need to stop. People are looking. And they'll gossip." The hot chocolate was darn good after an afternoon nap.

"I think that everyone already knows I'm infatuated with you. First I can't seem to stop following you on the set. Then I bring you this treat. Finally I'm singing love songs on your RV steps. I think the facade is set, don't you? Got to make it believable."

Stacy nodded. Somehow, she preferred her version that he found her tempting and couldn't help flirting with her. Instead he broke it down in a logical way. She hadn't bothered to consider what he would get out of helping her. Publicity she could guarantee him. Many of the teen magazines liked to feature her because of her penchant for designer clothing. The exposure wouldn't hurt his climb up the entertainment ladder.

"Any hints on how we'll start tomorrow?" Stacy asked to direct the conversation.

"I wrote a very brief outline because I want it to seem natural. I like getting the subject to open up and share. You never know who you might inspire with the unexpected information you reveal."

"I'm not sure how far I want to open up, though. I have to do the standard interview for the studios. But the other reason is to work to derail Antonio's plans."

"I'm a friendly ear. Why don't you run by me what you plan to talk about, and I can give you my opinion on what we may need to tweak?" Omar prompted.

"I think it's important to state why we are having a press conference in the first place."

"You want to tell the world about the new man in your life," Omar teased.

"Bite your tongue. I think we should stick as close to the truth as possible."

"You mean admit that Antonio is trying to blackmail you by revealing facts about your youth."

Stacy studied Omar, who had walked into the tiny kitchen. He looked around until he had an aha moment and grabbed an empty paper towel holder. Holding it triumphantly in the air, he approached her.

"What do you plan to do with that?" Stacy didn't bother to hide the alarm in her voice. The mischievous gleam in those walnut-brown eyes hinted that he was up to no good.

"Take your mind out of the gutter. This is my microphone when I pretend to interview you."

Stacy nodded, with a chuckle. Was she being paranoid or expectant?

He plopped down next to her and leaned in with one hand behind her shoulders. His breath tickled her ear, and another nervous giggle erupted.

"Would you behave? I can't believe my future and image depend on you." Stacy pushed away from him to give herself room to think.

"I promise to be on my best behavior. Even my family would be happy to claim me."

"So it's not just Brenda you have that effect on?" Stacy made a face.

"Didn't mean to sound as if my family and I have issues. Just the regular things that siblings squabble about. How are you with your family?"

"Don't have much of a family. It's me!" She threw out her arms. The declaration stirred her fear, along with her defenses. No one needed to know the depths of her loneliness as an only child with no father, a mother long missing in action and family members who opted for foster care when they couldn't take care of her.

"Only Brenda and the guys are my family," Stacy added.

"That explains the overprotective-mother routine."

Stacy raised his hand with the paper towel holder. "Let's get started."

The next morning, Stacy awoke early and headed to the set. Seeing Omar and Brenda awaiting her added support to her backbone. She could do this.

"We're ready," Omar mouthed. Discreetly he squeezed her hand.

This offensive strategy had to work. As she entered the area, the doubts nagged at her. Maybe she should have insisted that she talk to Antonio. After all, Antonio was the only one who knew her secret. Maybe somehow she could reach some tender part of him. Otherwise, he would tell the one thing that could reopen wounds, reawaken the pain and ignite the guilt for more than herself. No one could help. She placed a nervous hand over her stomach and walked onto the lighted stage where Omar waited and took her seat opposite him.

The cameraman signaled from the corner at the precise moment the light flashed, indicating that it was time to begin.

"Welcome to a special edition of *What's Happening in Atlanta*. I'm your host, Omar Masterson, and today, joining me in Montreal, Canada, is the beautiful, talented Stacy Watts." Stacy widened her smile and forced herself to relax. "Stacy, I know that you're a busy lady these days with lots of projects."

"Yes, Omar, thankfully I'm remaining gainfully employed." Stacy laughed, as they had rehearsed. She provided details of the movie experience and production details.

"What you've accomplished can only be called impressive. You are truly a role model."

Stacy hesitated, trying to remember how she was supposed to respond with the proper opening. One look at the camera lens, and her mind went blank. Frankly the thought of telling thousands of viewers about very personal things froze the connection between her brain and her mouth.

"A childhood friend has been threatening you about very personal things," Omar prompted.

"Oh, yes. I must clarify that someone who used to be a friend has decided to make money by telling lies about my childhood."

"Has this person done so already?"

"He has threatened me and sent me an advance copy of what he will sell to the tabloids and other media."

"Why not ignore it?"

Stacy stared into the camera. That much she remembered to do. "Because it is important to the fans that they hear the truth from me." She wasn't lying. And she meant every word that she would say in this interview.

"Then here's your platform, Stacy. Have your say." Omar reached over and squeezed her hand. Now *that* wasn't planned. But she welcomed his touch; it added some warmth to her cold fingers, clutching and unclutching her long skirt.

"People have made the wrong presumption that my background is a mystery. Far from it, my childhood has been a mixture of highs and lows, mostly lows. I choose to keep a forward focus. And now I feel someone is punishing me for that philosophy."

Omar leaned forward, looking into her eyes. "You have thousands of fans out there who believe in you. You are their inspiration. Some have probably chosen the entertainment field because of you. And sometimes, having a difficult childhood makes you more empathetic, a better survivor and no one's doormat."

"You flatter me." Stacy tried to read Omar for sincerity. Only yesterday, they had rehearsed. Yet there seemed to be more feeling in his delivery. "Let's see. Where to begin?"

"Where were you born?"

"Jacksonville, Florida."

"Family?"

"Lots of aunts, uncles and cousins." Stacy fought to keep her tone upbeat. "After my mother left the household, I lived with various family members." She cleared her throat, trying to diminish the lump that lodged there as tears threatened to surface. "I also lived in a couple of foster homes."

"Sounds like you had a tough life."

"In a manner of speaking. It was tough, but it prepared me for my life today. Not everyone has my best interests at heart."

"Did some of your experiences include incidences with the law?"

Stacy shook her head. "I wasn't necessarily one who only crossed the road when the Walk sign was lit. I did just enough to keep the girl gangs from kicking my butt on a daily basis, the boy gangs from making me a notch in their belts, the beat cops from harassing me in their street sweeps."

"When did you leave Florida and why?"

"I knew that I would leave Florida. Despite my life, I couldn't stop dreaming big. I worked odd jobs, lots of waitress jobs, then I entered a couple of high-profile contests and Brenda, my manager, spotted me."

"So Brenda was lucky enough to be in the right place to meet you. I'm sure that any manager would have made a mad dash to sign you."

Stacy heard the dig behind Omar's words. She imagined that Brenda was probably gnashing her teeth at his obvious dissing of her. "You might be right, but I don't believe that you can be matched with just anyone. Brenda came into my life at the right time. She helped me become a strong woman. I respect her for that." She had to make him understand that she wouldn't pick sides in their war.

"I concede your point." Omar raised his hand in mock acceptance. A crooked smile played across his face. "Your life doesn't sound so dark and mysterious. What was this person going to say about you?"

"Antonio Perez has been in trouble with the law at various times of his life. We grew up in the same neighborhood. In the beginning, he protected me, but then he took that protection to mean that he owned me. Once he made that decision to be in the business, I cut my ties. It was another reason for me to leave Florida and get my act together. Another reason why Brenda means so much to me."

"Did he come after you?"

Stacy nodded. Her throat felt dry. She licked her lips, wishing that she had a glass of water to drink before continuing down this rocky slope. Omar was deviating from the script. The grim set of his face didn't hide his anger. She didn't need him to get emotional about Antonio. He was old news. What she had gone through was old news.

"Did he hurt you?"

Stacy shook her head. From the glint in Omar's eye, he looked as if he would like to rip Antonio's head off. He had to hold it together, just as she did.

"I guess not until now, with his current plan of action."

"You could say that." Stacy tried to get Omar to refocus. "And I have you to thank for giving me this opportunity to connect with my fans before they are thrown ugly lies."

"Well, this Antonio person had better watch out because not only do you have thousands of fans supporting you, but I'm squarely in your corner." He took her hand and kissed her palm.

The camera swung from her on to Omar, who grinned with boyish enthusiasm.

Stacy could only stare. Omar had just shot off into orbit with that declaration. He'd gone solo on their plan. And once these cameras were off, she'd rip off his head, then hand him over to Brenda.

There wasn't supposed to be an announcement about him. He was simply going to be at her side at public functions. He didn't need to place his lips on any part of her body. She certainly didn't need to giggle and blush like a silly schoolgirl. Being around Omar made her think of the gravity-defying roller-coaster rides. She'd fasten her seat belt if she had one.

Chapter 3

Stacy turned her head away from Omar. She smiled sweetly into the camera and blew a kiss to the lens. "Well, it was nice talking to you."

Once the cameraman signaled that film had stopped rolling, she shot off the chair. Brenda was racing in from one of the corners. All their cell phones were ringing or buzzing. There would be a lot to answer for.

Brenda pointed toward Omar. "I warned you about this wannabe cowboy. Now he's ruined everything. There wasn't supposed to be an announcement. You were simply going to escort her to a couple functions, have the paparazzi take some photos of you together, get in the magazines showing Stacy as moving on with her life. Now you made it into your deal." Brenda stepped in between Omar and Stacy. "You'd better believe that you are not dumping Stacy."

"Didn't plan to." Omar remained seated with a stupid grin, as if completely removed from the situation.

"Miss Watts, you're needed on the set in thirty minutes. Makeup is ready for you."

Stacy turned gratefully toward the production assistant and followed her out of the set. Any place but on that soundstage suited her. Omar had made this an even bigger mess. She hated to think that he'd planned to do this all along. Was that the only reason that he'd taken the assignment? Although he didn't know about Antonio, was this a publicity stunt?

"I'm right behind you because I need to talk," Brenda demanded.

"I won't be able to answer you while I'm getting made up."

"I don't need your response. You need to listen to me."

They all crammed into the tiny makeup trailer. The interior had two chairs and lots of counter space. Various makeup containers, hairpieces and other accessories littered all the empty spaces. Stacy didn't care for the tight, windowless quarters.

Under the attentive hands of the makeup artist, Stacy surrendered to the application of heavy, thick foundation. With eyes closed, she tuned in to Brenda's speech; she hadn't paused since she'd begun voicing her displeasure.

"Stacy, are you listening? This is important."

Stacy gave her a slight nod.

"Send this guy back to wherever he came from. You're on your way up. We don't need any ripples in our journey. Antonio is a problem, but I'm not too concerned that we can't muzzle him. But this guy, Omar, is more of a threat."

"Why?" Stacy asked, wanting to hear Brenda's reasoning.

"How can you ask that when you were lip-locked with him?"

Stacy flinched, more than a little embarrassed at Brenda's remark in front of the makeup artist.

"Ma'am, can you relax your eyelids?" the makeup artist requested.

"Sorry," Stacy mumbled, forcing herself to comply, while Brenda continued.

"Honey, could you give us five minutes?"

Stacy opened her eyes, surprised to see the makeup woman heading out the door with Brenda giving her an apologetic smile.

"Five minutes," the makeup artist reminded her.

Brenda's reply was to close the door. Then she turned and faced Stacy.

"Brenda, you're exaggerating. And I don't have time for a long discussion about something that we all agreed to do."

"I didn't agree to anything. I caved to your pleading. But as usual, I'm here to clean up the mess."

"As usual? I have never been a problem to you. You have taught me well, Brenda. I don't take your advice lightly. You have to admit that we didn't have too much to work with, especially when we only have a short time to head off Antonio. Don't worry about Omar. I've got him figured out. Okay, I shouldn't have kissed him, but maybe that was more out of curiosity. It's not like I've dated since I signed on with you."

"And is that a priority? Men will always be there. No need to get distracted. Good grief, Stacy, think. Be strong. You're about to make a big wave with the upcoming album and this movie role. I'm expecting more scripts to come, but you've got to keep your image clean. Clear your mind of this high school nonsense."

Brenda had a point. Maybe she had used her impulsive nature to nab Omar for this inconvenient episode. But obviously she couldn't maintain control after things got rolling. This man whom she considered a sort of friend now had levered a wedge between Brenda and her.

"Brenda," Stacy called. "We always said that you can't turn back the clock. My past is a part of me that continues to haunt me. I know that the past haunts you, too. I'm sorry for being a constant reminder of your loss."

"Child, stop that nonsense." Despite Brenda's protestations, her voice cracked. "What happened with my daughter has nothing to do with you. As much as I miss her, I have to learn to live without her. But in you, I see so much promise. Maybe I see you as my second chance. But I'm also a good manager and I know how to protect you in this unforgiving profession. There will be time for flirting and courtship, all of that young-people stuff."

"We're a team." Stacy hugged Brenda tightly. There wouldn't be time to talk once the makeup woman returned.

"Ma'am, I have to get back to Miss Watts," the makeup artist said tentatively to Brenda.

Brenda exited the trailer, and Stacy could begin to mentally prepare for her role. Unfortunately, her movie part imitated life. The same memories and experiences she'd rather not deal with now had a function; she had to use the pain as a source from which to tap.

When the production assistant yelled her name, she scrambled to put on her costume as a homeless woman. With her makeup on and looking ten years older, she was on set thirty seconds before her scene started. Taking her place on a park bench, she let the rejection, abuse and self-loathing she had experienced wash over her. As the emotions sprang forth, her body posture changed, hunched over, her expression drawn downward. When the director screamed, "Action!" she uttered her dialogue in street dialect.

With the interview over, Omar extended his stay for the next two days. He'd convinced his boss that he had some things to wrap up. Now he wasn't sure what he should do. His adrenaline had returned to normal, and logic had its own voice. He couldn't believe what he'd done on live television. An apology didn't seem sufficient for the amount of damage that he might have caused.

He waited on the set, hoping to speak to Stacy. No outside persons were allowed into the soundstage. The only available place was the conference room, and, frankly, the thought of sitting there, on Brenda's territory, didn't appeal to him. From his out-of-the-way spot, he gathered his paperwork and equipment. Maybe he'd head to his hotel and call Stacy for a chance to explain himself. The time could help him sort out his feelings and provide a coherent explanation for his behavior.

"Don't think you're going to run off just like that."

Brenda's words doused him like a bucket of frigid water. His hands stilled in their task of gathering his note cards.

"I can only imagine what you must think of me," Omar started to explain.

"Let me explain something to you that I'm sure Stacy would not have told you."

Omar retook his seat. This time, she sat in his interview chair and he sat where Stacy had been as she answered his questions.

"Don't bother interrupting," Brenda ordered.

He nodded, puzzled that Brenda no longer seemed angry. She looked sad. Frankly the change in her demeanor unsettled him more than if she had simply called him names.

Brenda turned away from him. "I have been in this business for over twenty years, working in every position imaginable. In that time, I married twice, both ending in divorce. I decided not to go for a third time, figuring that it was a divine sign that I'm meant to be alone. From my second marriage, I had a daughter. Her name was Valerie. I'd call her Val. She was my light. I spoiled her rotten, but I wanted to be both mother and father for her. I didn't want her to be in need of anything or have to go beyond our family unit for anything.

"As she grew older, I stopped being her hero. I no longer impressed her with my hip knowledge and the latest dance moves. I became the dense, unappealing mother who kept her away from a normal life with friends. In her mind, her father had left to get away from me. Her hanging with the wrong crowd turned out to be the least of my worries, as she grew bolder with her disobedience. Then her options grew more dangerous. She ran away from home whenever I got tough with her."

Brenda pulled out a tissue and dabbed at her nose. She allowed the tears to stream. "One night, she left and never came back. The cops looked, but she was a habitual runaway and now seventeen years old. But I didn't give up. She was my baby. I tracked down every lead, learned what these young girls go through on the streets and cried every night as I thought about what she might be facing. One of the things that we'd fight about was my management company. She wanted to get into the hip-hop business. She had a voice and probably could have turned into something worth listening to with studio work, but the odds were against her. I wanted her to get an education and live a fairly normal life, then maybe consider the business.

"A private investigator told me that she was in Miami. I started going to talent shows and contests in that city. Instead of catching up with her, I had the chance to see Stacy battling with another rapper. She was so good that she put her opponent to shame and won the competition easily. I was impressed, but not enough to stop looking for Valerie. Plus I figured if Stacy was that good, she would appear at other contests.

"Everyone in that community talked about Stacy. She looked good, sounded great and had earned her props on the street. I found myself seeking her appearances and seeing the rough gem, waiting for the right touch. This meant that I had to go up against her then-manager, Antonio. Boy, he wasn't happy to see me, but I wasn't intimidated. He was a punk who took advantage of people. I knew that Stacy would blossom under my care.

"Once in a while, I ache for my daughter's return. But I have learned to move on with my life. I know that there is a reason that Stacy entered my life when she did. She is more than my client. Stacy is like a daughter."

There was a lengthy pause. Omar waited, half expecting to hear a threat against him if he ever hurt Stacy. It was the usual threat a big brother or father felt compelled to give when he showed up to take out his latest date.

"I lost one daughter. I won't lose another." Brenda picked up her pocketbook and stood. She brushed her cheeks and looked down at her wet hands. "I'll be seeing you, I suppose." She walked toward the door, and just before exiting turned to face him solemnly. "Take heed of what I say. I won't lose another."

Omar couldn't leave after Brenda had unloaded her bombshell. Instead, he sat outside the sound-stage waiting for Stacy to appear. He had no idea when filming would be done. His stomach growled, announcing its displeasure that he'd skipped dinner. The thing he did know was that after all that information, he wanted to be with Stacy.

"Yo, my man, when are things going to wrap up in there?" Omar got the attention of a young man hurrying from the building. The man's arms were laden with a large prop that he couldn't identify.

"They just did the final take." His voice strained under the burden.

Omar waved his gratitude, not wanting to hold up the young man any further. His mood lightened now that Stacy could emerge soon. Leaning against a nearby trailer, he whistled a nameless tune into the cool night air.

Finally the doors opened. Actors and staff noisily poured out into the parking lot. Apparently, the production was supported by a large number of people. In the semilit area, positively identifying anyone, specifically Stacy, proved to be somewhat difficult.

"Stacy!" Omar pushed away from his temporary waiting area and headed toward the familiar figure.

"Omar?" Stacy finished up a conversation with two other women before turning her attention to him. "What are you doing here so late?"

Omar pulled a bouquet of wilted flowers from behind his back and offered his biggest grin. "A peace offering."

She didn't take the flowers, but continued walking toward her trailer.

"Thought you'd be out much earlier." Omar ruefully noted the curled edges of the delicate petals.

"I'm at work," Stacy scolded.

"And it's definitely not a nine-to-five." Omar buried his nose in the floral bunch. "These are wilted."

"Then you'd better get them in some water." Stacy reached her trailer and turned to him. "It's late and I've got to grab a few things. Then Brenda is taking me to the hotel. I have another interview in the morning." She turned and opened her door. "By the way, I'm allergic to lilies."

"Give me another chance and I'll get you something that you'll like."

"Maybe." Stacy started to close the door.

"I'd like a chance to talk to you."

"Not tonight."

"I agree. It's late. Where's your interview tomorrow?" Omar refused to be put off by her ready dismissal.

"I'll do this one alone," she declared matter-of-factly.

"I'm supposed to be your boyfriend. I should be at your side since I'm here in Montreal."

"You have your job and I have mine. No one is expecting us to be together all the time," Stacy argued.

Omar took another whiff of the flowers. "These flowers need a home." He offered them to a passing older woman. She took them with a wide smile when he proffered a deep bow.

"Guess you've done your good deed for the day," Stacy said.

"I'll let you get your rest." Omar turned to leave. "But we do need to talk at some point."

"At some point," she echoed.

Omar gave up, but only for tonight. He hadn't acted with malicious intent. Plus she had proposed this bizarre scenario. He looked over his shoulder to see if she had closed her door. He was not disappointed to see her in the doorway, looking at him. "You know, I'm not the enemy," he shouted to her.

"I'm staying at the Royal Canada Montreal Hotel, but meet me here at seven. Don't be late." Stacy closed the door before he could reply.

But what would he say? His heart betrayed his cocky retort and reacted with a grateful leap. Heading to his hotel for the night wasn't so bad; knowing that she was staying at the same hotel was even better.

Stacy awoke early the next morning when the sunlight pried a blazing path between the heavy hotel drapes. After her shower, she read poetry by Maya Angelou and ate a bowl of oatmeal.

By six-thirty, she was dressed and waiting in the lobby, which was surprisingly busy given the early hour. Some of the production staff were also heading out. A few who recognized her waved. The principals stayed in another hotel that would cost what she earned from the movie. She accepted a ride to her trailer with the makeup artist. She was already looking forward to seeing Omar.

"What's got your attention?"

"Where did you come from?" Stacy jumped, startled to see Omar next to her. She had been gazing at the brisk pace of the area waking up.

Omar stepped up beside her. What a pleasant sight he made at the beginning of the day. He was enough to get her creative juices flowing. All he had to do was keep his wide grin in place and he charmed her. But she wasn't called stubborn for nothing. She didn't plan to join his female army of converts.

"Good morning," she greeted him with a smile.

"You're in a decidedly better mood." He squeezed past her through the narrow door frame of the RV and popped a kiss on her cheek.

"I have to finish getting dressed. I got a fab dress from the costume department, a mere loan, you see. Have a seat." She hurried to her room where her hose lay across the bed and two pairs of shoes awaited her attention. She must remember to send the wardrobe ladies a thank-you gift.

"I bought you a pound of Jamaican Blue Mountain coffee," Omar said.

"I don't drink coffee."

"What? You've got a coffeemaker."

Stacy laughed. "That's for Brenda or Fred. I don't do caffeine. Makes me too wired. I like to feel in control. Chocolate is a downfall."

"This means that I failed again with my bribes."

Stacy pulled on her hose, hating the feel of nylons against her legs. She was a pants type of girl, choosing dresses and skirts only for church. However, as a movie actress, she wanted to wear stylish designer clothing.

She looked down at the two pairs of shoes. Grabbing one pair in each hand, she walked out to the front where Omar studied the bag of coffee.

"Hey, you want to help me make a decision?" Stacy nodded to the small sitting area. "Don't know which ones to wear to the interview."

"Which would you like to wear?"

"Neither. I'd rather wear flip-flops." Stacy wrinkled her nose at the thin heel on the black shoes and the wedge heel on the red ones.

"I'd say go with the flip-flops. It'll make you seem approachable, youthful, not stuck-up. Qualities that I found attractive when I first met you." He approached her and held up one of the shoes. "This is definitely not you. Stay real."

Stacy weighed his advice with what she knew Brenda would say. She glanced at her watch. There wasn't much time to ponder this issue. She really wanted to wear the flip-flops, too. The first thing Brenda would remind her of was to think of her audience. She was going on one of the local channels for a few minutes to plug her upcoming album.

Sighing, she set down the black shoes and slid

her feet into their strappy confines. Her toes protested, then her calves joined in. How did women manage to put themselves through this torture?

"You don't take my flowers. You refuse my coffee. And now you dismiss my wardrobe choice. You're hurting me." Omar clutched his chest and winked.

Stacy shrugged and stuck out her tongue at him.

"Careful, don't send out invitations unless you're ready to party," Omar said with a drawl. "Guess it's time for us to go?"

They walked out together to where a car waited. The driver popped out as soon as they emerged. Stacy did the introductions and then climbed into the sedan with Omar sliding in close to her side.

Stacy settled back as the car entered the rush-hour traffic on the main road. Her arm brushed against Omar as the car jostled them. He sat much closer than necessary, but she didn't complain. His body warmth felt good against the morning chill.

Omar broke the silence. "Do you miss home?"

"Not really. I have an apartment condo that could be called home," Stacy answered.

"I know what you mean. I'm like that, too. Home has turned out to be wherever I'm at for that time." He took a deep breath and looked out the window. "A bit sad that Montreal won't be home, though." Omar craned his neck to look as they rode through the old city.

"Because?"

"I'm due back in Atlanta by tomorrow. That means I'll be leaving you."

"Oh." Stacy hadn't thought about his leaving. She guessed he did have to go back to work. "Are you still interested in…um…being my boyfriend?"

Omar took her hand and intertwined his fingers with hers. Stacy admired his hands, strong, blunt-fingered, not soft but certainly not rough. Maybe they had seen some hard work. But she'd guess that he probably found an alternative that required less sweat.

"You think too much," he said.

"I've been accused of worse. But using my brain has saved me."

"Is this where Antonio had a part?"

Stacy nodded.

"Tell me about him," Omar coaxed.

"Let's wait until after the interview." Stacy made a small motion with her hands. "It's important that I'm thrilled to bits with my life during the interviews."

The sedan turned into a lot where a guard waited. Once the driver took care of the details, they were allowed to enter. Omar hadn't let go of her hand. She took that as a good sign.

Once the door opened and her feet hit the ground, she was swept up with the television staff. Brenda was already in the building talking with the host. Omar followed behind the crowd. Once in a while, Stacy peeked at him behind the frenzy of assistants. He didn't look abandoned as her conscience had needled her. Instead, he looked very interested in the entire goings-on and the plethora of females who were as busy as termites around him. Maybe it was her only-child status, but she wasn't into sharing even if he was her fake boyfriend. If they were still around after her interview she'd have to snatch a few women bald.

Omar didn't have to look up to sense Stacy staring at him. She didn't look pleased, especially when the women smiled and flirted with him. Little did she know that he wasn't interested in the superficial nonsense of model features, brickhouse curves and flirtatious foreplay. He wouldn't say that he'd grown out of appreciating the sexual dynamics. But he was much more selective of with whom he'd play. None of these women could compare to Stacy, neither in physical beauty nor classy personality.

At that moment, Stacy stepped onto the small

stage set designed as if for a fireside chat. Omar studied her as she was fitted with a microphone. Her thick, luxuriant hair shone under the lights. Her wide cheekbones reflected the exotic mixture of her ancestry, which he was sure had a little Native American in it. It would be only a matter of time before she replaced the so-called sex symbols. Then some hypersexed teen would share his admiration of her full-figured body.

As she shared her journey to being discovered with the host, he listened to what she said, but charged to his memory all that she didn't say. That was why he considered her a complex but alluring woman who left so much to be discovered.

And he wanted to learn what turned her on.

Chapter 4

Stacy looked down at the long, white envelope in her hand, wishing that she didn't have to play messenger. She took the remaining pile of mail from the kitchen counter and hastily laid it on the coffee table in the family room, hoping that the letter would give some comfort to her manager.

"What you got there, kiddo?" Brenda entered the kitchen, heading past Stacy for the family room. "Thanks for bringing in the mail. Probably all bills." She wrinkled her nose and ran her fingers over the mound of envelopes, setting aside a few to be reviewed more immediately.

"What time do we need to get on the road to make the concert?" Stacy deliberately tried to focus Brenda's attention on their plans to take in an outdoor neo-soul concert to celebrate her completion of the movie part and their return to Atlanta.

"We can leave now and that will give us time to get a good parking spot." Brenda's voice drifted off. Her hand hovered over the envelope. Slowly she picked it up and opened it. Stacy saw her shoulders rise and lower from her deep, audible sigh. She'd hoped that maybe Brenda would wait for a private time to read the contents.

Feeling uncomfortable as an unwilling witness, Stacy moved out of the room and took a seat in the living room. All she heard was a slight rustle of paper. No sound of weeping came from the room. She read that as a good sign.

"It's from Valerie."

Stacy nodded.

"She said not to worry about her." Brenda refolded the letter and set it down on the side table near the door. "Not to worry." She laughed, a bitter sound. "Still no clue as to what a mother feels."

"I'm sure she said more." Stacy saw the frustration and anger in Brenda's scowl. "It'll get better. She obviously wants to keep you informed," she coaxed, hoping that Brenda could see the positive aspects.

"It's like a wound that keeps being reopened."

"I'm not going to let you believe that, and you don't really feel that way. I would want to know how my daughter was doing, even if I couldn't see or speak to her."

Brenda gently touched the folded letter. She looked up with unshed tears. "Guess you're right." She stood silently, clearly taking a few minutes to collect herself. "We have a concert to enjoy."

"I'm right behind you." Stacy hurried through the front door as Brenda engaged the security system.

Stacy maneuvered through the neighborhood. Kids in small groups strolled down the street toward the community playground. Adults jogged and biked along the sidewalks. More conscientious residents washed their cars or mowed their lawns. Brenda chose a radio station of classic oldies. But Stacy couldn't resist needling her and changed the station to the number-one-ranked R & B station. She turned up the volume in the upper-crust community, and got tickled with the looks of displeasure as Ludacris and L'il John rapped their raucous lyrics.

Stacy finally gave in to Brenda, who covered her ears.

"Not in the mood today."

Stacy drove a few more miles before Brenda

blurted, "She wants more time to think. But she thinks that one day she'd be ready to see me. Soon."

"I know it'll be soon," Stacy encouraged. She had become Brenda's rock through the ordeal. "Let's go and have a good time."

Forty minutes later, they arrived at the Chastain Amphitheater, joining the hundreds of others sharing in the outdoor extravaganza. People from all backgrounds and ages gathered in lines leading into the park. The community of fans broke down barriers as people turned to each other to carry on animated conversations.

Once they were inside the park, the swell of people became chaotic. Those with tickets for the lawn seating rushed to get their prime spots. Stacy had called in a few favors to be seated in the middle lower-front rows. She hoped that Brenda could return home in a mellow mind-set after enjoying the concert.

"Thanks for this," Brenda whispered.

"It's a small thing that I can do to say thanks," Stacy answered. She'd love to do more to show her gratitude. Maybe she could help with reuniting mother and daughter.

As the various bands warmed up between sessions, Stacy headed to the concession area to purchase two slices of greasy pizza, sodas and pretzel bites. By the time the main act came onstage, they were happily munching. Stacy figured she'd eat now and exercise later.

Brenda suddenly leaned in close to Stacy. "When are you planning to see your fake wannabe boyfriend?"

Stacy chose to keep her attention on the soulful young singer. It had taken her manager two hours to ask what clearly must have been weighing on her mind like a megaton truck. Ignoring Brenda's pointed stare, Stacy snapped her fingers to the catchy riff. When the singer led the group to raise their hands and sway to the melodic crooning, she followed suit.

The song ended before Brenda started in on her again. "I'm only asking from a business manager's perspective."

Stacy hooted at the false declaration. "Guess we're done talking about Valerie."

"I don't trust either of you not to have cooked up a change to the plan without consulting me."

Stacy reluctantly turned her attention from the last song, one of her favorites. The finale drew a thunderous roar from the crowd. "Stop staring at me and at least enjoy the last song, please," she prodded.

Brenda's nagging didn't cease on the way home.

"I'm dropping you off and I'm not coming in," Stacy declared. "You'll have to pick my brain some other time."

"I'll tell you what was in my letter if you tell me about that man," Brenda wheedled.

"That man is Omar," Stacy replied crisply.

Brenda shrugged.

Stacy didn't really need to know what was in the letter, figuring that was between Brenda and her daughter. Knowing Brenda, the offer to share meant there was something important that she might share.

Stacy pulled up in front of the house. She noted the dark interior. Brenda hadn't left on any lights. The all-brick minimansion stood dark and looming on the slight hill.

"I'll come in for a few minutes." Stacy turned off the engine.

At least twenty years stood between Brenda and her. Yet they were both single with their own demons to conquer. Maybe that's why they got along. Loneliness was the underlying theme in their lives. This fact motivated Stacy to stick around for Brenda's sake.

"Care for anything hot?" Brenda headed for the kitchen, turning on the various lights as she walked through the house.

"No, I don't think I can eat or drink anything

else. All that junk I ate has me stuffed." Nevertheless, she followed Brenda and sat at one of the bar
stools against the dining counter.

"Valerie promises that she is okay. That she's
working out her life before she can see me again."

"Oh, Brenda, that's wonderful news, isn't it?"
Stacy walked over and hugged Brenda. "She's
trying to get her life together. I know that must
have been uppermost in your mind."

"I'm not the kind to hang on to empty promises.
But since Valerie left, I will listen to anything,
live on hope, even light a candle in the window."
Brenda idly wiped the kitchen counter. "However
long it takes, I want to see my baby." Her voice
shook slightly.

"Valerie will appreciate your support." Stacy
hurried over to Brenda, who was hunched over,
head bowed. Her manager was a proud woman
who hated to have witnesses to this one thing that
seemed to buckle her at the knees. Stacy rested her
forehead against Brenda's head.

"Some days are better than others when I can
believe in miracles." Brenda pushed away. "What
about your young man? I mean Omar."

"As a matter of fact, Omar has moved into a
new condominium. He invited me over tonight,
but…" She shrugged. Never mind that saying no
had practically made her ill.

"I can handle Omar. And I'm not being naive. We're enjoying each other's company. It's been a while since I've had a male friend who makes me feel comfortable."

"You're on your way up. Why have the dead-weight?"

"Better question is, why do you hate Omar so much?" Brenda's accusation pricked Stacy's dignity. "You know what, I think we'd better say good-night and leave it at that. We had a nice evening. I'd rather your prejudices against Omar didn't cloud it."

"I've never seen you lose your head over anyone like this."

"And that should tell you a lot. Look, I'm tired of defending my personal life. Let's agree that it's off-limits." Stacy grabbed her car keys and left.

Her anger had gotten the best of her. But more than that, Omar with all of his sex appeal and hunky good looks had certainly scrambled her good sense.

Her cell phone rang. She glanced down at the lighted display, expecting to see Brenda's number. Instead the number displayed was new to her. Her hand hovered over it. Once in a while a fan would get through to her on the cell phone. She waited for the call to be kicked into the voice mail, hoping that the caller would leave a message.

Stacy pulled into her condo parking lot, maneuvering through the underground garage to her reserved spot. Cell phone reception didn't have a chance two stories below the surface. Her caller's message would have to wait until she got up to her condo.

Inside, she dropped her keys on the side table. Her shoes already lay strewn on their sides. On autopilot, she turned on her stove and placed the kettle on the burner. While the water boiled, she pulled off her clothes, opting for a lounging top and pants. Only then did she get her phone and retrieve her messages.

Omar had to admit that he was disappointed that Stacy didn't pick up when he called. He had to work late to finish an entertainment piece for the station. He'd hoped to be able to coax her into coming over, despite her earlier rejection. But his plans had changed.

He was pumped with the plan he had in mind. The execution, on the other hand, gave him a slight queasiness. All the possible objections to his idea had gone through his head a million times. A new employee who worked with the company for less than a year, who didn't know all the ropes, now had an idea. He could imagine the backlash.

Nevertheless, the doubts didn't stop him from

holding his appointment with Ted Henderson, his immediate supervisor. His anxiety mirrored his emotional state at his interview. Even Mr. Henderson's secretary wished him luck, since she had to reveal the reason for the meeting before making the appointment. He adjusted his clothes before knocking on the door, blowing out a nervous breath.

Once Henderson granted him entry, Omar gulped at the luxurious office furnishings. The size and features were a little less than phenomenal. Maybe he should've worn a tie and dress slacks. One minor comfort was that, if Henderson tossed him out, most of the employees had left at five, although gossip only needed one nosy soul to spread like a virus.

"Mr. Baxter?" Omar didn't mean to sound so incredulous that the CEO and president of UTP was in Mr. Henderson's office. "Good morning...I mean, afternoon." Why shouldn't the head of the company meet with his employees wherever he pleased? "Good afternoon, Mr. Henderson." Remembering whose office he was in, Omar addressed his immediate boss.

"Young man, it's evening. What are you doing here at this hour?" Baxter asked. He sat on an overstuffed sofa off to the side where a small meeting area was staged with a sofa and two armchairs.

"I had to finish a write-up for next month's

show. And I like to get started on my upcoming projects to keep a handle on everything."

"Smart man you have here, Henderson." Baxter's face didn't crack a smile. Instead, Omar suffered under his scrutiny as if he were being assessed with the final verdict withheld. "I always judge a man by how many times he checks his watch and how fast he skips out of work at the end of every day."

"I agree. Omar has been doing a fantastic job with our aggressive push to get that younger audience. And the women love him," Henderson said.

Omar shifted uncomfortably.

"Those other stations have their hosts decked out in gangsta-style clothes, looking like hoods on the loose. I'm glad that our people are savvy enough to go for the high-fashion style with a little touch of street." Baxter wore a shrewd expression. His fingers tapped a rhythm on the sofa arm.

"Well, Mr. Baxter, Omar is meeting with me to share a few of his ideas. Would you care to stay? Looks like we may have a visionary."

Omar offered a tight smile, unsure whether his boss was making fun of him.

"I'm listening. I'm impressed by any employee willing to take risks by telling the man who signs his paychecks that what he is doing isn't good enough." Baxter drilled him with one of his famous stares. His dark eyebrows drew blunt, thick lines over penetrating dark eyes. Everything about the man was blunt. His features, body shape, even mannerisms had a powerful impact. He pointed to the chair across from him.

Omar accepted the silent invitation, preferring to have a sturdy piece of furniture to support him.

"I was throwing around some ideas with the programming goals in mind. We have the music-video angle, interviews and a few town-hall meeting sessions in our lineup." Omar paused to check on his audience. Henderson and Baxter gave him their undivided attention. He continued. "I think that we should have TV specials where we go out and talk about the problems among the youth like a minidocumentary. Bring some awareness to common problems. At the end of the show, we could have viewers call in for help or counseling." Omar finished, his chest heaving as if he'd run a sprint.

What did they think? Would he be clapped on the back and allowed into the boys' club? Or would he be told that he had ten minutes to clear his work area?

Baxter stood. A big grin spread across his face. He looked down favorably on Omar. "I like how you think. Let's kick this idea around with the other departments, Henderson." He gripped Omar's shoulder, gave a brief nod and left the office.

Omar had never been around a person who could fill a room with his presence. Actually, as he thought about it, his brother had that ability. He hated to admit it, but the tension was more familiar than he'd have liked.

"That went well." Henderson looked at him minus the warmth. He returned to sit behind his desk. "We have a planning meeting in a week. I'll bring it up then." He picked up a few papers and tapped them into line. "Did you need something else?" Henderson looked at him as if surprised to find him still there.

"I guess I thought you'd want to get more details."

"Why?" Henderson asked, with a raised brow.

"When you speak to the others, they will need to know what the project entails for budget purposes." Omar saw something flash in Henderson's eyes—it couldn't be disinterest. "This is more than an idea."

"I bet it is. You're a young man working his way up the food chain. But paying your dues is also part of the game." Henderson stood.

Omar sensed the dismissal. With no other choice,

he stood, meeting his boss eye for eye. "I believe in this idea. I wish that you'd give it a chance."

Henderson escorted him to the door, patting his shoulder. "Don't worry about it. Your time will come to shine."

Omar followed the momentum of a gentle push through the door.

"Now it's time for you to go home. Don't overwork or else those great ideas will stop coming."

The great oak door closed in Omar's face. "If you think that I'm going to give up, you're out of your mind," he said through clenched teeth. As he picked up his work for the evening, he thought about going straight to Baxter's office. At least he seemed genuinely impressed with his idea. Maybe even the president was having a good laugh at him.

Omar went out into the night, his spirits dragging along with his footsteps. He drove through streets that teemed with nightlife. There was a time when he would have been out there ready to meet what Atlanta nightlife had to offer. Now he spent his evenings working on his career.

Recently his work ethic had become a bit inconsistent. He marked the change with seeing Stacy in Montreal. He'd tried to see her when she'd returned to Atlanta, but her voice mail was his only contact.

It was his habit to tell interested women that he would call them and then not do so, and he didn't much like the tables being turned on him.

One game had already been played on him tonight, one where he didn't accept the rules. He wasn't sure what he would do about it. And now Stacy played her own game against him. He refused to accept that, either. Now that he had a new plan, he changed directions and headed north. Before long he stopped at the gate of Stacy's closed community, awaiting entry.

Without warning, rain began to fall. Through the blurry windows, he could see the guard talking and turning his attention to him. He didn't have a backup plan if Stacy refused to meet him.

"Proceed, Mr. Masterson. Have a good night."

Omar saluted, much happier as the gates swung open. He drove through the neighborhood of single-family and condominium units. On his right he saw the community center. In the rainy darkness, the building's many glass windows were well lit. He could see the impressive gym equipment, a large flat screen and an area with small tables and chairs. The outdoor pool was expansive. Farther down the main street, there were a row of tennis courts and an equal number of basketball courts. "Must be nice," he muttered.

As he approached Stacy's home, he spotted her standing at the entrance waving at him. She was casually dressed, making him wonder if he'd roused her. Another disturbing thought popped into his mind. What if she was entertaining another man? He didn't feel that secure given his circumstances with her.

"Thanks for seeing me," he greeted.

"I've been incredibly busy, but I got your messages."

"I know what you mean. I've been working late almost every night." Omar struggled to act nonchalantly.

He entered her home, a little surprised to see it simply furnished. Stacy didn't strike him as the type to get too done up about anything. But the unit appeared underfurnished, as if she lived there only temporarily.

"May I fix you a drink?"

"No, thanks, I need to keep a clear head. Have an early morning ahead of me." Omar studied the photos on her bookcase. The children in the photos were the same as the ones in her trailer.

"My niece and nephew," Stacy clarified from behind him. "I'll fix us some hot chocolate, okay?"

Omar nodded, then sat on a small love seat. The apartment had an open floor plan. He admired her as she made hot chocolate. Her hair, in relaxed curls, was loosely bound. Her tank top defined her figure, providing only a thin barrier to his imagination. Her smooth brown skin glowed under the fluorescent lighting. Even without makeup, she had a natural beauty that didn't need to be concealed or disguised.

"Do you need any help?" Omar inquired. Mainly he wanted to be in that small space near her.

"Nope. You relax. I'm guessing from those yawns you've tried to hide that you had a hectic day at work."

He nodded, looking slightly embarrassed. Despite her reassurances, he walked toward the kitchen. He leaned against the entranceway. "Yes, I had a very hectic day. No, I didn't come to lay down my burden."

"You don't strike me as that type of man. But I am a good listener," Stacy bragged before handing him the mug.

"Delicious. I love marshmallows," he said appreciatively.

"I'm glad. Looks like you needed a little comfort food."

He set down the mug, none too gently. The liquid sloshed over the side, but he didn't move to clean up the spill, nor did Stacy. He looked into her face, not knowing what to say that wouldn't scare her. His mind fumbled through some sort of comment that would share some of the turmoil he felt. She needed to know how much he thought about her, how much he wanted to talk to her, how much he wanted to be with her.

Stacy walked toward him and stopped only inches from him. She placed a hand in the middle of his chest. Her touch warmed the spot and the warmth radiated all over his body. His breath hitched as she slid her hand up toward his neck. He bit his lower lip to stop the groan that could embarrass him.

"May I ask you something?" Stacy asked in a husky whisper.

Omar could only gulp in response.

"Do you want me?"

"Yes," he hissed. What was this woman trying to do to him? He closed his eyes, squeezing them shut to block out the kitchen light, her beautiful features, her soft botanical scent. He wanted to be a good, honorable guy with his barely concealed crush.

"Would it help if I told you that I wanted you?"

He nodded.

"Then let me make love to you all night long."

His eyes opened to see her smiling up at him.

Chapter 5

Omar's muscles twitched under the soft pressure of Stacy's fingers kneading his chest. She placed her cheek against the warmth, listening to the hurried thump of his heartbeat.

She tiptoed up to kiss the corner of each side of his mouth. His lips opened in welcome, but she only wanted to tease him with a sample. There would be time to trace the outline of his lips with soft kisses of her own.

"You didn't call me," Omar accused under a strained voice.

"If I had called, I would have begged you to stay."

"Instead, you used me for the moment."

She bore his hurt scrutiny. As an apology, she kissed the indentation at the base of his neck. His Adam's apple bobbed repeatedly.

"I won't be distracted, but you can kiss right here." Omar pointed to his chin.

Stacy obliged. "You wanted more from me than I was willing to give." She hovered with her ministrations. "Let's talk about this later." She took his hands, wide and strong, and placed them on her hips. When he gently squeezed her hips, a tantalizing spike of sensuality coursed through her body.

His hands slid a little lower, cupping the curve of her behind. She inched closer, pushing away any part of reality that would kill this moment.

She pulled her tank top over her head and let it slide down her arm. With all her bold moves, it took great effort not to cover her bared breasts. His unabashed desire celebrated her femininity. Her nipples promptly hardened with an invitation all their own.

"Take me to my room," she commanded breathlessly, her pulse racing.

He complied, lifting her in his arms. She curled up against his chest as he made his way down the hallway. She pointed toward her bedroom.

He lowered her gently to the bed among the

large number of cream-and-burgundy pillows and
stuffed animals. She was less lonely surrounded
by their softness. Many nights she fell asleep on
the couch, wrapped in a blanket, the TV cutting
the darkness and empty silence.

"Stacy, I'm not sure about this."

Stacy stopped tossing the pillows off the side
of the bed to look at Omar. Conflicting emotions
played on his face, a mixture of bewilderment and
suppressed interest. "Don't be afraid on my
account. I want this, don't you?" She knelt before
him, unbuttoning his shirt.

His taut muscles provided a perfect landscape
of pecan-brown that stretched along the ripples of
his chiseled body. She traced the peaks, feeling the
hairs bend to her will. His breath hitched as she
circled his nipples and drew a line down the
middle of his stomach to his belly button.

"I want you more than anything, Stacy. But if we
do this, act on impulse, then we prove Brenda right."

Stacy paused in her delivery of feathery kisses
on his shoulders. "This is not the time to think
about Brenda, or any other woman, for that matter.
Don't you believe I know what I want? What I
feel? You can't tell me that you don't want to lie
here with me."

"Yes, I want you." Omar lowered his head and
kissed her so deeply that no part of her remained

unmmoved. "I've thought about you since you suggested that I go after this job. You gave me a hand when I was struggling to find out what I wanted to do."

"You give me too much credit." Stacy moved up the bed and slid under the covers. She refused to let this moment slip away.

"I wanted time to court you. You didn't give me that chance."

"Why are you talking like an old-fashioned guy? Courting! Why are you doing a 360-degree change on me? You didn't strike me as the type who waited for the starting gun to sound," she replied. All this talking didn't help.

"You're different."

She tapped the space next to her on the bed. "Come show me how different." She raised a hand to stop him. "And I don't want to hear about Brenda while I'm trying to get my groove on."

Omar finally sat next to her, but he didn't touch her. "I have a three-date rule."

"And that means…what?" Stacy frowned, waiting for an explanation.

"I date at least three times before going…further."

Stacy blinked, hoping to wipe away any images of Omar in a tight embrace with another woman. The thought soured her mood. "Omar, has any woman ever objected to or tried to change your rule?"

"Nope." Omar smacked his knee. His male ego practically oozed and bounced off the walls around them.

"Let me enlighten you. I'm in charge. This is my place and this will be on my terms." Stacy pulled her panties off under the blanket and then held them over the side to drop near Omar's feet. "Now, don't keep me waiting."

"This is new."

"I know, big boy. You're used to sitting in the driver's seat delivering your high-octane sexuality in your conquests." Stacy tossed the blanket aside. "I've wanted to do this to you for a long time, since I first got to know you. I'll slow down long enough for you to jump aboard." She grinned. She was nervous, but unafraid to lie side by side with this handsome, thoughtful man.

Omar finished where she had left off and slid his shirt off. Obviously he cared about his body because not only did his chest and stomach show proof of a weight-training regimen, but his biceps bulged and tapered down to strong forearms. If she was with her girlfriends, she would appreciatively refer to him as a young stud, standing half-naked in only black cargo pants and black hiking boots.

He finished undressing under her brazen observation. Stacy didn't make the moment any easier for him. Instead, she propped herself on the pillows and waited as if she were Cleopatra on her royal chaise. When he stood in only his underwear with his hands cupped over his arousal, she giggled like a teenager.

"You know what they say about payback, right?" Omar said in a low, husky voice.

Stacy nodded. "I can hardly wait. But in the meantime, I have some scented massage oil in that drawer." She indicated the small nightstand beside her bed.

"You *were* ready," Omar remarked.

"I was working up my nerve. But then you popped up at my door." Stacy sat up and pulled her hair into a loose bun before turning onto her stomach. "We'll save the best for last." Then she settled in place, fully anticipating his first touch on her naked skin.

"Towels? We might get messy." Omar followed her hand signals to the area in her closet dedicated to the linens.

He retrieved two beach towels and spread one under her. When he made no move to touch her, she looked over her shoulder. He stood near the windows, turning the shades so that the room dimmed. Then he turned off the light, leaving only the bathroom light, and, with the door partially closed, it satisfactorily muted the brightness. One last adjustment and they'd be set. She turned on her CD player. Once the heavy bass pounded through the speakers, she hit the button to eject. This was not the time for booty-shaking, raucous lyrics. She thumbed through her old-school pile and selected Anita Baker. This was the time to use crooning love songs as a backdrop for the real thing.

"You're making me work too hard for this," Stacy said, as she settled back into position with the blanket loosely covering her behind.

"You can't rush quality."

With those words, Omar's hands, lathered with oil, lightly brushed her back. He moved around her entire back as if his fingers wanted to learn the nuances of her physique. Meanwhile, the light pressure caused goose bumps as her body primed for his sensual touch. She groaned appreciatively, too lazy to form words of appreciation.

"I feel some tightness here." He circled an area on her lower back. "And here." His hands slid southward. Stacy drew in a trembling breath. "Oh, and here." His fingers stroked the top of the split in her behind. "But I'm sure that I can relax it with a little of this." His hand rubbed the fullness of each cheek. She fought the urge not to bite her pillow. She couldn't play the queen and then crumble at the first onslaught to her nervous system.

After he had paid the proper amount of attention to her lower back and beyond, he provided her legs with long, skillful strokes. The deep pressure was the perfect solution, since she had worked out particularly hard on her treadmill.

"Right there," she directed, approving his technique on her ankle joint. "Gosh, you're good. Didn't expect an expert, but I'm not complaining."

"I've got a few tricks. If you had given me my three dates, you would have learned all about it."

Stacy turned over onto her back and stretched with a slow, liquid grace. "Hmm…you're going to be a stickler for your rules on dating." She traced a line down the center of her body, trailing her finger between her breasts and over her stomach. She paused over her belly button and granted him her widest smile. "You are Omar Masterson. Youngest sibling. Women love your big brown eyes. Men hate your fine good looks. You are slightly afraid of your big brother, Pierce. You're used to having your own way. Only your sisters can push you around, or baby you with their attention."

"Not bad." He bathed her leg with the scented oil, gliding his hand up the side of her body and over the top of her chest.

Stacy swore that her eyes crossed for a few

seconds before she could regain focus. Two could play at this game. She reached for his hips, acknowledging his muscles tightening beneath her fingers. Casually, she brushed her thumbs along the sides of the dense, coarse hairs, a forewarning of where her hands would go next.

He bared his teeth and uttered a decidedly wicked hiss before a dangerous smirk crossed his face. He lowered his mouth to her breast, tasting her with an intense ferocity that lit up her insides. As he connected with her breast, she craved a similar connection between her thighs. The thought had her blushing.

When he nudged her legs apart, she obeyed. Her body lay poised, aching for the initial contact, sensitive and moist for his entry. He paused for a second too long. She wrapped her legs around his hips, interlocking her ankles, and arched up to meet him. No sooner had they touched than he buried himself deep within her, as if no further introduction were necessary.

The music set a beat for their primal rhythm. Stacy ground her pelvis to meet Omar's thrusts. Their grunts and moans punctuated the air in the master bedroom. She turned her head into his cheek, enjoying the roughness of the evening stubble along his jawline. Their mouths met in a tangle of lips and tongues overladen with passion.

Some part of her wanted a moment to catch her breath. Another part of her didn't want to break contact merely for a chance to breathe. As Omar drove deeper into her, she gasped at the peak of climax. She shut her eyes tightly, twitching with each wave matched by Omar's spasms. All of his massaging was wasted as her muscles locked until they were both spent.

In his arms, she slowly drifted back to reality, her head spinning. She'd never equated satisfying sex with an appetite, but after that workout, she wanted a juicy piece of steak and thick, fat French fries smothered in ketchup. Omar tightened his arm around her and she decided that food could wait. There were other matters that warranted her attention. She smiled up at Omar. He groaned in mock protest. But a small smile tugged at the corner of his mouth.

The next day, Omar sat in the restaurant booth, waiting for Stacy to return from the restroom. There was a fairly good crowd for lunch that had caused them to wait for forty minutes to be seated. Stacy had been pretty adamant that she wanted to come to the steak house. Besides, he was hungry, too. Coming here together after their marathon lovemaking session would give them time to talk.

"Ordered the drinks yet?" Stacy slid into the seat across from him.

Omar nodded. "Just need you to decide on your entrée."

"Don't need a menu." Stacy tapped her temple.

Just then the waiter returned with their sodas. Omar placed his order while Stacy quenched her thirst. Based on his intimate knowledge of her size, he guessed that she was a grilled-chicken-with-steamed-vegetables type of woman. He personally wasn't going that route and ordered the highly advertised surf-and-turf platter with his steak done medium well.

Stacy winked at him, then turned her attention to the waiter. "I'm going to have the Hearty Fisherman's Platter."

"Fried or broiled?"

"Fried, of course." Once the waiter left again, she turned to Omar. "I've had to eat veggies and salads for the past six months for the role. Now I'm going to splurge."

"I didn't say anything." Omar raised his hands and winked.

"Give me a break. I saw the look in your eyes, as if you could see the pounds practically glue themselves to my body."

"Only looking out for your arteries," he remarked, half jokingly. He couldn't help himself.

His mother's early death from a heart attack was forever etched in his memory. "Forget I said that." Where did that sad thought come from? As the youngest, he hadn't had the advantage of his mother's care and attention in his teen years.

In good time, the waiter returned with plates that covered most of the table surface. Omar's mouth watered from the rich, seasoned aromas.

"I really am sorry that I didn't contact you when I returned. I wanted to, but Brenda…" Stacy dropped her fork onto the plate. "What am I saying? Look, it wasn't Brenda. Not that she's thrilled about our friendship. I didn't call because…well, darn it, I got scared. I hadn't been with a man since Antonio. And that ordeal wasn't the model for loving relationships."

He liked her honesty. She threw it out there with a challenging tone. If she only knew that in the beginning, he'd felt that he was moving faster than he was used to doing. No woman had ever captured his interest with such intensity. Along with that realization, he had a growing sense that he wanted this long-term.

"I'd say that we got what we deserved, a fresh start." Stacy smiled enigmatically from behind her glass.

"To our fresh start. May there be many more in our future." Omar raised his glass and tapped hers.

"Hear hear!"

They finished their meal with a heated discussion of what football teams would make it to the Superbowl. Funny how at one time, he'd preened over his title as a ladies' man. Suddenly that seemed so superficial. Stacy's depth of knowledge might not be academic, but she exhibited such intelligence about a wide variety of matters. He enjoyed speaking to someone who was his equal, rather than someone whose only interest was in being a short-term distraction.

"Now I'm stuffed." Stacy pushed away the plate and groaned.

"Let's go for a walk."

"Walk? Are you crazy? I need to lie down and catch up on my sleep."

"You'll thank me for the walk. There's got to be a park nearby where we could get in a fifteen-minute walk.

"I'll decide on the thanking part when I'm done." She wrinkled her nose.

"Then let's go." Omar signaled the waiter, paying the bill as quickly as he could.

He didn't have far to drive before he turned into an upscale neighborhood, guessing that it would have a walk path around a common area. Sure enough, there was a man-made lake with the required small paved path circling it.

"This is absolutely gorgeous," Stacy exclaimed, hurrying out of the car before he got a chance to open his door.

He followed her running steps toward the path. "Could you slow down before I keel over?"

"Oh, so now you want to take it easy," she shouted over her shoulder.

Omar could hear her faint laughter despite the wind carrying off its full effect. Always up to a challenge, he pushed to catch up. He'd just discovered another thing about Stacy. She was either a past or a current runner. Unless she took pity on him soon, there was no way that he would be able to catch up.

He passed a large flat-topped boulder on his right. Bingo. He veered off his course and sat. Stacy hadn't turned around yet. He hoped that she wouldn't disappear around the corner before noticing that he wasn't following. Other runners and speed walkers passed his rest spot. Could they look less pleased with themselves? He'd like to meet them all on the tennis court. It had been a while, but he was sure that he could still serve a few aces.

"Hey, slowpoke." Stacy approached from behind, a huge grin in place.

"I got caught up with the surroundings and wanted to admire."

She sat next to him, chuckling. "Thanks, I feel better."

"Good for you," he replied irritably. He wished that she would stop giggling. "I drove us here. So I can leave you here, if you don't show a little humility."

Stacy cleared her throat. "Sorry. I'll be good. Want to split a stick of gum with me?"

Omar accepted her peace offering. He couldn't have planned this any better. Spending an afternoon in the park with Stacy was a better treat after the meal than any dessert choice.

"Ready?" Omar stretched his back. The boulder, although handy, was not exactly comfortable.

"Back to reality, huh?"

Omar nodded.

"What are your plans for tomorrow? Think you can get away for lunch?" Stacy asked.

"I'll certainly make the time. The job has irked my nerves to the limit." Omar briefly shared his frustration with Stacy. "I'm not going to take that mess."

"Yeah, well, I guess they want you to pay your dues. Look at it from their point of view. You're a young kid." She raised her hand at his protest. "I know, I know. In their eyes, you're their sons' age. And here you come with your ideas when they have been at it years, making mad money." She playfully nudged his knee with hers. "Your time will come."

"First, you sound as if you're a hundred years old doling out advice. Second, the president liked my idea. It's my boss who had an issue." Omar kicked at a pebble. His irritation was barely submerged.

"Want to share your idea?" Stacy prodded.

Omar shook his head. He stared out at the park, not really taking in the outdoor scene. Why set himself up for another pat on the head? Now that he was ready to step up and be a man with a plan, someone was there to flick their finger and knock him back down.

"Then let's go." Stacy rose from the seat and walked past him.

Omar grimaced, sensing that Stacy was miffed that he'd cut her out. He jogged to catch up. "Hey, didn't mean to come off so cold, but I don't think you understand how unfair it all is."

She didn't answer. They headed back to the car.

"I'm not trying to tell you what to do," Stacy said. "I'm only talking from my experience. Everyone expects you to pay your dues. You don't have to sell your soul, but the faster you realize that this is what people expect, then their reaction doesn't come as a surprise." She turned in her seat to face him. "I promise not to laugh at anything you tell me." She crossed her heart and held up her hand.

Omar laughed. "It's not a big deal. I think that a series of minidocumentaries geared to teens and young adults would add some balance to the current programming of music videos, celebrity reality shows and other popular shows. I want to provide beneficial information and resources for kids in trouble."

"I think it's wonderful. No, actually it's darn brilliant." Stacy smiled a wide, approving grin. "Don't let your boss get away with dismissing your idea so easily."

"What happened to the paying-your-dues soundtrack?" Omar teased.

"I just figured that you might have been asking for the window, the corner office." She punched his arm.

They arrived back at the restaurant for dinner. A new crowd had replaced the twelve o'clock lunch group. From outside, Omar could see that three suits sat in the booth he had shared with Stacy. The timing was perfect.

"This was a good eating spot," Omar said. "Next time, I'm taking you to my favorite hangout."

"We'll see." Stacy backed away from him. "I

haven't turned over the steering to you yet." She blew him a kiss and then tossed her hair over her shoulder before sashaying down the sidewalk.

"Riding shotgun may not be so bad at all," he muttered under his breath. His eyes never shifted from her receding great figure before she turned the corner. Omar took his shades out of his pocket, slipped them on, jammed his hands in his pockets and strolled toward his job.

There were some afternoons when you just had to say whatever. The day was great. Lunch was great. His girl was great. He'd have to rethink that one. If she was playing head pilot, then she should be asking him if they wanted to go together. He pulled out his cell phone and dialed.

"Hey, Omar."

"Got a question," Omar said.

"I'm listening."

"Shouldn't you be asking me to be your steady beau?"

"I thought that was already established."

"Nope. I'm feeling the need for more than a one-night stand." Omar ignored the curious glances as he walked and talked on his cell phone. What did he care if they heard? They'd never see him again.

"The more you give, the more they want." Stacy gave an exaggerated sigh. "Stop by tonight and I'll make it official."

Omar grinned with the unexpected plans for the evening. This was truly a beautiful afternoon. He could sing in the rain, snow, hail or sunshine and perform his own tap dance of happiness.

Stacy snapped the phone closed, pressing it to her lips where a soft, dreamy smile played. She added a bounce to her step as she entered the office building to meet with Brenda.

She practically sang an afternoon greeting to the secretary. Looking at the time, she surmised that she had four hours before Omar's arrival. After catching up with Brenda on a few items, she would have the afternoon to herself.

"Stacy, have a seat."

Brenda finished her conversation on the phone while Stacy opted for the edge of Brenda's desk. She was too wired to sit still for long and took to pacing in the office. A light pop tune came to mind and she hummed unashamedly as she stared out of the expansive office windows. The traffic below zipped through the maze of buildings like busy bees on a mission. Some days she simply wanted to retreat from the hectic pace and ponder anything but what she was obligated to do.

"Earth to Stacy, what's got your attention wrapped so tight?" Brenda came over and stood next to her.

"Nothing much. Wondering what you've got for me." Stacy tried to keep a certain level of enthusiasm in her voice.

"How would you like to lend your voice to animation? A project is already in progress." Brenda held both hands up for a high five. When Stacy didn't respond, her hands slowly drifted down to the desk.

"I'm excited, but I want to hear more details. I don't have a particularly special voice."

"Stop that nonsense. You have a powerful voice. I remember that young girl at the Open Mike in Little Havana. Small body with a powerful voice. You had everyone eating out of your hand. When you sing and rap, your attitude changes," Brenda said. "This is great exposure, Stacy. It's what you wanted."

Stacy tried to push her way through the objections that quickly came to mind. For one, she didn't know why she should have reservations. After all, there were probably bona fide celebrities who would love to have their legacy permanently marked by a children's animation feature. "Who is backing this film?"

"The company that produces a lot of the shows on the Children's Cable TV Network."

"What's the character?"

"A girl who wants to be a rapper, rebels and

wants to quit school to follow her dream. Don't you think it's ironic?" Brenda asked.

"Did they know about my background?" Stacy frowned, ready to go after Brenda if she had told this company any of her personal history.

Brenda shook her head.

"I don't want to play this role. What's the challenge in that?" Stacy started to explain her doubts, but thought better of it. She had to concentrate on what really bothered her about the project. Then she'd have to convince Brenda.

"I don't think that I'm hearing correctly. This is a good opportunity. Different. Fun. Hip."

"Stop saying that word to me." She leaned forward, her frustration clearly revealed. "I don't want to be a hip-hop anything. It's what provided me with food and shelter, but it's not me."

"Do you think your fans would let you off so lightly? They would make an example out of you for betraying your roots as soon as success touches your feet."

"My roots!" Stacy's face flushed with all the anger and frustration that she kept barely buried.

"Yes. Whether you want to recognize it or not, your life is a hip-hop story. For circumstances beyond your control, you were shunned, rejected and abused by people who took advantage of the system. Yet, you stood in the middle of all the muck because of a strong survival instinct. You wouldn't be denied even when you were with Antonio, who was only interested in keeping your wealth flowing to his pocket. All these facets of you have people enamored with you. You can't turn your back on them. You're breaking the contract you have between you and them."

"Oh, don't sound so dramatic, Brenda." Stacy stamped her foot in annoyance. Brenda always managed to argue her point so well, and the eventual result was always that Stacy would fold her protests and follow along.

"Take this home. Read it over and get back to me before eight in the morning. I'm sure that you will come around to seeing my side."

"Brenda," Stacy began slowly, "when you encouraged me to leave Antonio, that's all it was—encouragement. I made the decision for better or for worse to sign on with you. Over the years, I have not come to regret it. But I do have a mind of my own." Stacy picked up her pocketbook. Her mouth was dry. Her hands shook. Her legs felt positively weak. She gritted her teeth and headed for the door. "I'm prepared to walk, if you won't listen to me."

Chapter 6

Stacy ignored Brenda calling her name. She wanted to escape the office, the building. She hadn't meant to lay down an ultimatum. Brenda was everything to her. They'd never had such a volatile exchange in any of their dealings. But she felt trapped, suffocated, with no one who listened to her. Her opinion didn't seem to matter. Stacy entered the waiting elevator, knowing that she'd have to apologize for her behavior.

Despite the nosedive to her day, she still had several appointments, including one for her hair. Pushing back her emotions was not difficult for her. She'd learned to do that most of her life. No one cared what she thought or felt as long as she didn't disappoint. Antonio had certainly drummed that motto into her head, first with words, then with a frequent shove and finally with the palm of his hand. She remembered the first reminder that had stung for hours. He'd comforted her that it was tough love, especially since he'd consciously kept his hand opened and not curled tightly into a fist for her benefit.

When rough times tested her limits, she sucked in her feelings and pushed forward a perky, happy veneer. The facade seemed to be coming undone. After completing a couple of errands, she checked her cell phone. There were no messages or missed calls. She was a little unsettled that Brenda hadn't called. Knowing her manager, she was in a fine temper.

"Can't believe you're on time," Veronica, her hairdresser, shouted from her station where she finished the final touches to a client's hair.

"I'm always on time." Stacy took her seat in the waiting area.

Despite the hustle and bustle of the hair salon, this was the perfect place for her to spend a few hours. No one cared who she was. She'd joke around with Veronica, get caught up on the gossip in her life and argue about the next style for her hair. She pulled out her cell phone again. No incoming calls.

"Girl, come on back here. I'm ready." Veronica, who stood at least six inches higher than Stacy, peered down at her head.

Stacy hadn't bothered to do anything special with her hairdo since she was coming to the hairdresser.

"Looks like you need a touch-up. I told you about waiting until this much new growth has come in. You're breaking your hair." Veronica parted her hair, inspecting the roots, voicing her strong disapproval. "You're lucky that you've got such strong hair. Otherwise, you'd look like a bald eagle. But keep it up and you'll be wearing a wig."

Stacy went through the painful process of relaxing her hair. Despite the mild version and the heavy dab of petroleum as her base, the process still stung. However, she had no desire to go natural. Brenda occasionally tried to convert her, but such a change didn't appeal to her.

Veronica led her to the shampoo bowl. Stacy made herself comfortable and leaned back for one of Veronica's famous hair-washing and massage treatments. The temperature of the water was perfect. She relaxed in the chair and enjoyed Veronica's magic fingers. The water rushing down her hair and around her ears into the washbowl soothed her frazzled nerves.

"Don't make me beg. Fill me in. Where have you been?" Veronica moved her fingers from the edges of Stacy's hairline to the center of her head.

"Nothing to fill in. I'm back in town. Have a few pending endorsement deals. Preparing to get to work on the next album. Hoping that I can get a couple of weeks off to do some navel-gazing and contemplate life."

"Not interested in the boring details," Veronica quipped. "Did you hook up with any young brothers on the set?"

"Maybe."

The rush of water stopped. Stacy opened her eyes to see if Veronica was finished. She hadn't yet applied the moisturizing cream for the deep conditioning. Veronica's dark eyes stared back at her. Her mouth pursed in a full pout.

"Don't get huffy at me. I could have just not said anything." Stacy smirked. The remark earned her a douse of cold water. She shrieked. "You are so evil."

"Better start talking. My other client just came in."

Stacy filled her in about Omar. She left out the forced arrangement, but shared how much she loved being the driver in the relationship.

"Sounds like a big wuss." Veronica's lips curled

with distaste. "Me, I like my men a little on the rough side. Keep the choirboys at home." Veronica smacked her lips and grinned.

"Whatever! My man is no wimp, wuss or mama's boy." Stacy took her seat under the hair dryer, prepared to spend the next twenty minutes as the conditioner penetrated the hair shafts. Chemical processing and the necessary hair therapy were long, tedious exercises.

Two hours later, Veronica swung Stacy's chair to face the mirror. The curls hung loose and shiny, framing her face. The hairdresser had added gel to the front of her hair, sweeping it partially over her forehead. The style dropped a few years off her face. Although she wasn't planning to hit any clubs tonight, she looked forward to Omar visiting her this evening.

Her cell rang. Figuring that Brenda might be calling, she slowly open the phone and looked down at the number. Instead, her nerves went into hyperspeed for a different reason. She hurriedly answered to hear Omar's voice.

"Hey, babe."

"Hey, yourself." She giggled, covering the mouthpiece with her hand. She sensed Veronica's stare on her head.

"I'm heading to a meeting. Not sure when I'll come out. Wanted to let you know."

"I'm at the hairdresser's. I'm going to have to battle the rush-hour traffic when I head home."

"Where are you?"

She filled him in on the address, and then her phone beeped, alerting her of another call. She excused herself and took it, recognizing her cousin's telephone number. "Hey, Sabrina."

"Need a quick favor. Got a date with this guy that I've been dying to go out with. I need someone to watch the kids. Please," Sabrina begged.

Stacy didn't want to be tied up all night with Sabrina's kids. But Omar might get caught up with work for most of the night.

"Stacy, you know I'd do the same for you."

"I don't have kids, Sabrina," Stacy replied, annoyed with Sabrina's tendency to live her life at each moment.

"Well, when you get a man and some kids, I'll do the favor."

"Fine!" While Sabrina was scatterbrained, leaning more on the selfish side, her son and daughter were sweethearts.

"Good. See you in an hour?"

"An hour!" Her phone clicked. Darn it, Omar had hung up. Her day had begun on the high road and spiraled down to suckville.

"Gotta run, Stacy. Whoo-hoo! Tonight is going to be a party night."

"May I remind you that it's not the weekend? You do need to come home at a reasonable hour. I'm not spending the night looking for you."

"Well, take the kids over to your place. I may not come home tonight. Then I can pick them up from you. Look, this is a wonderful way to see what it's like having kids of your own."

"I'll be there in an hour." Stacy had no desire to carry on the conversation any further. With her fabulous hairdo, she was no babysitter. Instead of buying a good bottle of wine, she now had to head for the grape and peach juice, fruit cups and frozen chicken nuggets.

"I think you'd better call your man back." Veronica held the hair spray two inches above her head and then pressed down on the nozzle. The choking cloud forced Stacy to close her eyes and hold her breath until some of the noxious fumes dissipated.

"I don't know why you try to kill me with that toxic stuff every time. My hair will look like a hot mess by the morning." Instead of Omar's hands in her hair while they tussled in a frenzy of lovemaking, she was about to have two kids playing with the curls, probably rubbing applesauce in it. Then she'd fall asleep in an exhausted state to wake up with hair like the Bride of Frankenstein.

"Call that man now." Veronica finally put down

the hair spray, but didn't back off. She stood with her arms folded, waiting for Stacy to obey.

"He was going to a meeting," Stacy reasoned.

"Then leave a message."

"What am I going to say?" Stacy listened to the phone ringing.

"You want him to come over."

"With the kids?" Stacy stared at her.

"Of course."

"That's one sure way to get rid of a man," Stacy protested.

"Girl, hush up. It's a way for everyone to be relaxed because nothing heavy can take place. Kids aren't going to judge him or want anything from him. It's also a nice way to check him out around kids. See if he's got a sensitive side or is even playful." Veronica nudged Stacy with her hand. "Especially if he's a serious thing for you."

"Still think that he'd rather go see a chick flick than be roped into babysitting," Stacy replied stubbornly. She'd witnessed too many dramas of single mothers in the dating scene.

"He's a wuss. He'll do it without a complaint since you're wearing the pants."

"Hey, ladies, I hope I wasn't the topic of that conversation." Omar grinned at Stacy's stunned expression.

"Omar!" Stacy shot out of the chair, threw her

arms around his neck and pressed her body against him. "I can't believe you're here." Then she remembered that she'd told him where she was. "You're sneaky."

"Thought I'd surprise you. Don't have long though." His arms loosely lay on her waist.

"Ahem. Folks, this is a G-rated place of business. Take the steamy stuff elsewhere. Of course, that's after you introduce me to this handsome gentleman." Veronica sized up Omar, who was nonplussed at her bold gaze.

Stacy made the introductions. "I'll go pay now." Stacy headed for the cashier, expecting Omar to follow. Instead Veronica hooked an arm in his and pulled him to one side. Stacy made quick work of paying and providing Veronica with a sizeable tip. Her hairdresser had been with her for over five years. Back then she'd paid Veronica for her services on an installment plan. They'd hit it off when Veronica was a student and Stacy had decided to try her hand at being a manicurist. At the time, being an entertainer was only a dream.

"Omar, are you ready?" Stacy didn't trust her hairdresser not to say something outlandish to Omar, although she might already be too late to stop it.

Omar said his goodbyes and walked out ahead of Stacy. Stacy followed him, grateful that they could escape prying eyes and gossipy tongues.

She looked over her shoulder at Veronica, sensing her hairdresser's watchful gaze.

Veronica gave her the thumbs-up. Stacy couldn't stop the smile. Her man was no wimp. As he continued strutting out of the salon, many women stared over the top of their magazines at his retreating rear. One bold soul spoke up, "Girl, I ain't mad at you. You got it goin' on."

Stacy couldn't agree more with the woman's comment. Her professional life might be a ball of confusion, but in her personal life, there was a sense of contentment. She slipped her hand in his as she guided him toward her car.

"This was a great surprise," she said.

"Thought I'd drop in." Omar looked at his watch. "But I really must rush back. You were so close, I couldn't resist." He kissed her lips softly. "Can't wait for tonight." He grinned, mischief twinkling in his eyes.

Stacy groaned. "You won't believe what I've gotten roped into doing." She didn't wait for him to guess. "I have to babysit my cousins."

Stacy didn't like the way he studied her with open curiosity. "If you are up to it, you can join me," she invited.

"Where will you be?"

"At my place. I suspect that I'll have them all night."

"What are their ages?"

"Six and eight. Boy and girl."

"You owe me—big."

Stacy nodded, secretly thrilled that he didn't run for his car, never to be heard from again.

"I'll see you tonight, then." He pulled her against his body, resting his hands on her behind. "Guess I'd better get this in now since we'll be in G-rated company later this evening."

She nodded with full support from her entire body. She tiptoed up to meet his beautiful mouth. He lingered over her lips, kissing the curvature of hers with tantalizing softness. Stacy wound her arms around his neck, molding her body against his, eliminating any space left between them. She opened her mouth, welcoming his deeper kiss where their tongues connected.

A beeping sound jarred the moment. Stacy opened her eyes, lips still locked with Omar. Life's activities flooded their intimacy. The brightness of the day, the sounds of traffic, the mixture of smells from area restaurants announced their presence.

"There's my watch alarm. Now I've really got to run." Omar kissed her forehead and then ran toward his car. "Sorry," he yelled over his shoulder before speeding up his retreat.

Stacy smiled, touching her lips where minutes ago his mouth had stroked them awake. She got in her car and immediately turned on the radio as she pulled out of the parking lot. Her mood soared with the heavy bass thumping through the interior of her car. Hair done, body tingling with sexual energy and the steady, rhythmic beat of reggae music, Stacy was in a good mood for her babysitting assignment.

Omar returned to the office, running into the conference room a few minutes late. His boss paused in his announcement, long enough to let him know that his tardiness was noted. Omar tried to look as apologetic as possible given the remaining headiness of his shared kiss with Stacy.

Omar listened off and on to his colleagues' status reports. He hoped that this wouldn't be one of those meetings where his boss would get off on a tangent, and two hours later, they'd be exiting the room.

"Mr. Henderson, I'll need an extension on my timeline for the before and after," a coworker said.

Omar cringed. The request seemed normal enough, but his boss hated to deviate from any plan unless there was a dire emergency.

"Mr. Hopkins, why are you costing me money?" Henderson asked. Omar would have treated it as a rhetorical question.

"Sir?" Lance Hopkins looked miserable. "Um...we

are having a problem getting the Spelling brothers to attend. They have a public feud."

"Then whose bright idea was it to get them in the first place?" Henderson raised his voice, his face suffused with anger.

The research team visibly shifted their bodies to tighten their cluster. The five-person team had to lean on their loyalty to the group. Omar understood their principle, but sensed that the philosophy would also be their downfall.

"Meeting over." Henderson ran his hand through his hair, leaving it stuck up like the top of a carrot.

Everyone scrambled toward the door. Omar had planned to make a more public pitch for his idea. Given the sudden turn of events, he'd wait. Someone else was about to be beheaded.

"Mr. Hopkins and the research team, stay put!"

No one turned, although shoulders visibly relaxed. Omar looked at his poor colleagues only after he left the room and was safely in the hallway. He could see his boss in a full-blown tirade.

"We lucked out," a relieved colleague remarked before heading to his cubicle.

Omar nodded, but didn't enjoy the thought that one day that would be him. It was just a matter of time. The difference was that he couldn't guarantee that he would sit quietly like a naughty boy in the dunce's corner. The others treated this dramatic episode as a rite of passage. Only his brother, Pierce, could get away with giving him a public tongue-lashing.

Omar sat in his cubicle and pulled out his writing pad. Before long he'd scribbled more notes about his idea. He needed to launch it with a powerful topic that earned the young audience's attention and also hand-delivered high ratings to his company. He tapped his pencil against his mouth, trying to figure out what would be the top five issues on teens' minds: drinking, drugs, eating disorders, online dating or the definition of sexuality.

All of these topics were overdone. He could practically see his audience rolling their eyes. Yet he knew that if he did touch a common problem, his angle had to be unique and compelling. He tilted his head back and stretched. An idea had taken hold. He had to make it happen.

"Hey, Omar, heads-up, the footage for your opening piece wasn't any good. Can't use it," the assistant editor stated.

Omar dropped his pad. His idea was now forgotten. This new predicament required quick thinking. He raced down the hall to the editing booth. Finding a solution was his mission. Finding one before his boss caught wind of the problem was essential.

Stacy walked into her cousin's apartment. Sabrina had opened the door and disappeared into her room to continue dressing. The entire place looked like a children's play den. Toys were strewn everywhere. As she inspected, she spied several cardboard wrappings of past meals.

"Where are my little cousins?" She loved her second cousins, even if their mom could be a scatterbrain at times.

"Fran! Lenny! Your aunt is here. Show some manners!" Sabrina screamed from her bedroom, before emerging with one shoe in her hand and the other on her foot. "Don't make me come in there to you."

Stacy raised her hand to calm the situation. Most of all, she wanted Sabrina to stop screaming. "How soon will your date be here?"

"I have to pick him up."

"Figures," Stacy muttered. Somehow, her cousin always seemed to select guys who needed something from her. "You're taking him out, then."

"Yeah. He's in between jobs." Sabrina poked out her head. "I can't pay you for this." She disappeared again.

Stacy went into the kids' room. They were engrossed in an action-adventure movie that she'd consider too old for them. "Hey, guys, where's my hug?" She slowly walked in front of the TV, earning a roar of protest.

She held open her arms and they promptly ran into her embrace, wrapping their small arms around her hips.

"Are we staying at your house?" Fran asked. A faint trace of whatever she'd drunk gave her a mustache. Her small pigtails were all askew.

Stacy nodded, earning another hug.

"Auntie, can we get nuggets and fries?" Lenny asked with a big grin. Obviously he knew that his cute smile was his selling point.

"Have you had dinner?"

They both nodded.

"Then why don't we have apples and cheese for a snack?"

"I only like red apples," Fran announced. She grabbed a backpack and started to stuff her dolls in.

"I hate cheese." Lenny's grin had turned into a ferocious frown.

"You don't have to eat cheese. How about yogurt?"

"Why can't you have good stuff to eat—like candy?" Lenny's mood didn't lighten.

"Well, you know I do have some treats, but no one gets anything unless you both are good. I have to be good, too. We are the Three Musketeers, right?"

"I don't want to be a mouse." Fran looked at her backpack with all the toys bulging out and threw it down with frustration. The zipper couldn't close.

"*Musketeer* is a soldier." Lenny finally smiled again, clearly proud of his knowledge. "I saw the cartoon."

Stacy moved through the room, gathering clothes for them. Most of the stuff she pulled out of the drawers was stained and smelled. Didn't Sabrina pay attention to what they were doing in here? Stacy went to the kitchen and grabbed a large trash bag from the box under the sink. Then she returned to the kids' room and shoved in as many clothes as possible. She'd wash as much as she could.

"Okay, I'm heading out. I'll call you when I'm coming home," Sabrina said.

"I'll keep them tonight. But you need to get them in the morning." Stacy looked at the youngest members of her family. They needed love and attention. She was willing to give them what she hadn't had.

Sabrina positively danced a jig in the hallway.

She celebrated her good luck by placing a call and sharing the good news. Plans were suddenly amended.

"I'm serious, Sabrina. Tomorrow morning."

Sabrina gave her kids a hug and kiss, blew a kiss to Stacy and left. Her trail of perfume left a significant marker all the way to the door. Stacy turned her attention back to her wards for the night. Their bright, eager faces stared back at her.

"I think we're all set." Stacy herded them out of the apartment and out of the building. "Oh, no! Your car seats."

"What car seats?"

"Don't you use car seats?"

"Sometimes. Grandma makes us sit in them all the time, though." Lenny didn't sound happy with his grandmother's rules.

"Very good for Grandma. That's pretty important and we can't go to my house if you don't have car seats." Stacy's mood matched the kids' unhappy expressions. She didn't want to stay in Sabrina's home. Besides, Omar had said he would visit. She wasn't expecting him for another half hour. Maybe she should call to let him know that the plans might change.

She approached her car, parked on a side street. Something appeared to be propped against it. The kids ran ahead. "Our car seats. Look, Auntie, we have car seats. Did the fairy godmother leave them?" Fran asked, looking around for the mythical creature.

"No, sweetheart. It was probably your mother. I'm sure that she knew we couldn't leave without them." Stacy could see Sabrina driving up, hurriedly setting the seats against her car and jumping back in to be on her way. She looked up and down the street, strangely empty on a Friday night. Thank goodness no one had helped themselves to the items.

"Kids, stop running!" Stacy kept the reminder on a continuous loop as they raced up and down her hallway. They liked the sound of their feet against the hardwood floor. "Time to eat your apples. Fran! Lenny!" They had been forbidden to go into her bedroom, but she could hear their giggles behind the partially open door. "I'm not playing hide-and-seek," she declared, a small smile tugging at her lips. She couldn't believe that she sounded like her mother, when she'd been around—and coherent.

"Come out, come out, wherever you are," she sang, as she noisily moved through her living room, dining area, kitchen and bathroom. Finally she moved into the bedroom and flipped off the light switch.

Two piercing screams came at her. She turned the light back on. "Gee, I didn't know you were in here."

"You need a night-light," Fran said. Her eyes were round and full of horror.

"She was scared. I wasn't." Lenny gave his sister a soft shove.

Stacy placed a restraining hand on his shoulder and firmly shook her head. "Have you had a bath?"

"No. Too many baths dry your skin," Fran declared with a matter-of-fact attitude.

"I want you to take your bath. I have lots of moisturizer for your skin. You've got clean clothes from the dryer. You're going to smell like a good little boy."

"Good little boys have a smell?" Fran questioned, her focus on her older brother. From the way she wrinkled her nose, she wasn't buying Stacy's line of thinking.

"Yep, and so do good little girls."

"I'm taking my bath first." Fran ran into her bedroom, already peeling off her clothes.

"Lenny, have a seat in the living room until I'm done with Fran. The remote is on the table. Only the kids' channels are appropriate for viewing."

Lenny nodded, then hurried into the living room to claim his spot on the couch.

Stacy took Fran by the hand and headed for the bathtub. The water gushed into the tub while Fran splashed with her dolls. The harried activity with the kids slowly demolished Stacy's hairdo. The curls had loosened under the bathroom's humidity. Now if she managed to stay dry, that would be an accomplishment. Fran continuously slapped her hands on the water's surface. Her girlish giggles proved contagious.

"Looks like you need a hand."

Stacy spun around, scared and surprised to hear Omar's voice. He remained in the hallway while her heart dislodged itself from her throat and settled back into place.

"How did you get in? I didn't hear the doorbell."

"I rang a couple of times. Then your nephew opened the door."

Stacy's mouth opened at the potential horror of such an innocent action. "How could I forget to tell him not to open the door or answer the phone?" She didn't want to leave Fran alone. She'd have to talk to Lenny later.

"You do your thing and I'll sit out here with Lenny."

Stacy nodded. Fran hadn't slowed down with her water play. Stacy soaped up a washcloth and scrubbed her little body.

"All right, little girl, you're all done. You can have a warm glass of milk and then bedtime."

"Warm milk is nasty." Fran grimaced, showing her baby teeth.

"Okay, cold milk." Stacy felt wilted around the edges. She had a nagging pain in her lower back since she'd spent the last half hour leaning over the tub.

Fran grinned and hugged her. Good, she'd received approval. Stacy sang familiar childhood songs and rhymes while she applied lotion to Fran's slim frame, then sprinkled cornstarch powder on her, before slipping on her nightdress. "Now you smell so good that I may not be able to stop hugging you."

After she had poured Fran her drink, Stacy headed for Lenny. From the look on his face, he wasn't going to head to the bathtub as easily as his sister. It was too late for any nonsense. She put on a stern expression.

Omar sat across from the little boy. He was teaching him how to move chess pieces on a board. Lenny leaned forward and whispered into Omar's ear. Then Omar nodded.

"Lenny has something he'd like me to say."

Stacy didn't take her eyes off Lenny. She crossed her arms and waited.

"Lenny feels that he is too old for you to help

him with a bath. He also doesn't think that you should see him naked. And he will call you if there is an emergency in the bathroom."

Stacy thought everything was reasonable. Yet she was a bit surprised by Lenny's adamant position. Maybe privacy was something that eight-year-olds protected at the pain of death. She stepped aside as he marched past her.

"There is a fresh blue towel on the rack."

"Okay."

Stacy hovered at the door. "If you need me, I'm here."

"Aunt Stacy, I've been taking showers on my own for lots of years. I'll remember to wash behind my ears and everything."

"Step away from the door," Omar whispered. "He isn't risking life and limb in there."

"What if he slips and falls? What if he hits his head?" Stacy imagined an increasing number of serious injuries that could happen behind the door. She shook her head. "Nope, I'm not moving."

Omar sighed. "I'll pop us some popcorn and then we'll sit out here and eat."

Stacy chuckled. "I know I'm being unreasonable, but I can't help it." She slid to the floor and sat with her knees drawn to her chest, listening to Lenny and smelling the scent of freshly popped corn.

"Aunt Stacy!"

Stacy jumped at Fran's call. She scrambled to her feet and ran into the bedroom. "What, honey?" She sat on the edge of the bed holding Fran in her arms.

"Could you leave on a light?"

"Oh, I forgot." Stacy went to the electrical outlet where she had a night-light already plugged into the wall. She flicked on the switch, which provided a soft, comforting glow. She stayed with the little girl until she fell asleep.

Then the silence hit her. Silence meant that the shower had stopped. She was supposed to be on watch. She eased her arm from under Fran, then ran into the hallway. The closed bathroom door didn't matter. She was going in.

Her hand grabbed the doorknob as it was pulled from her grasp. Lenny came out with a wide grin that showed his toothless gaps. "I like your shower," he announced as he walked past her.

Chapter 7

"Ever thought about having children?" Stacy looked up at Omar's face.

A large bowl of popcorn sat between them. The kids were down for the night. A bad movie from the eighties played on TV. In her way, she had managed family night. Stacy enjoyed the mellow mood in Omar's arms.

"I think that I'd like having children. We didn't have an easy childhood, but we had each other," Omar answered.

"Well, mine certainly had its memorable moments. Most of which I'd rather forget."

"Do you have a big family?" Omar stroked her cheek.

"Not really. A few did try to help out as much as they could, or at least that's the version I choose to believe."

"You don't sound bitter."

"I'm not bitter. Sad, maybe." If she admitted to any resentment, she'd sound ungrateful for how her life had turned out to this point. "One time I think life is short and I should do whatever I want. The next time, I think that I should be helping others not to endure what I did." Stacy leaned up. His eyes held her gaze, filled with empathy. As much as she felt safe with him, she wasn't sure that she wanted to share the darkest parts of her life. She heard the pride in Omar's voice when he talked about his family. What she knew existed in her past didn't hold up against his hearth-and-home lifestyle.

"Now that I'm working in a profession where I can excel, I wonder if I wasted too much time job-hopping. Unfortunately, I have such a shady reputation that my brother doesn't believe I will stick around."

"I believe in you." Stacy reached up and touched his jaw. She admired the strength in his face, the determination that shone strong. Omar seemed so consumed by his big brother's approval, she wanted to see him reach inward and draw on his own strength.

"That means a lot to me." He pulled her closer to his body, resting his cheek against her head.

They remained leaning against each other, lost in their own thoughts.

"Aunt Stacy, wake up."

Stacy stirred, wondering why she was dreaming about Fran. She tried to turn over and get more comfortable, but met with an impediment.

"Aunt Stacy!"

Stacy frowned, trying to get her thoughts in order. Then a doorbell rang and she came instantly awake. "Fran!" She sat up, rubbing her eyes. "Are you okay?"

"Someone's at the door." Fran looked at the door. She held on to Stacy's hand tightly. Unlike her brother, she didn't run to the door.

"Where's Lenny?" Stacy walked toward the door. The sunlight peeped through the curtains. She couldn't believe that she'd slept through the night. She looked through the peephole and saw Sabrina. She opened the door.

"Hi, cousin, looks like I woke you up." Sabrina stepped in, a little too perky for the morning. "Did my kids wear you out? Well, welcome to my—"

Stacy closed the door and turned to see what had interrupted Sabrina's enthusiasm. "Oh, that's Omar."

"Well, I wasn't the only one getting my groove on." Sabrina scooped up her daughter and peppered her face with kisses. "Where's your brother, sweetheart? Not sure that your aunt knows anything at this point."

"Omar and I fell asleep on the couch." Stacy couldn't imagine how she had fallen so deeply asleep. She must have been really tired. She tapped the top of Omar's head. He didn't need to look that contented on her couch.

"Yep, I'm up." Omar sat up and quietly stood when he saw everyone staring back at him. "Didn't realize you had company."

"At least his clothes are on," Sabrina remarked, before setting Fran down. "Sweetie, go get Lenny. Tell him that we have to go. Grandma is coming over this afternoon. We need to get the place straightened up."

Fran ran down the hall, screaming out her brother's name.

Stacy turned back to Sabrina, ready for her remarks about having Omar in her apartment.

"Are you going to offer a cup of coffee?" Sabrina walked into the kitchen.

Stacy followed her in, while Omar excused himself.

"Looks like you're keeping him a secret." Sabrina motioned toward Omar's exit.

"No, I'm not. He's my friend."

"Good for you. You had me worried that you were going for the old-maid routine. Just because Antonio was a jerk, don't let that stop you from finding a good man. That's my philosophy, anyway."

Stacy started the coffeemaker. She didn't want to have a discussion about Antonio. She'd rather not talk him into her existence, again.

"Well, tell me about your man," Sabrina said a few minutes later, as she poured herself a cup of coffee, took a long, noisy sip and pulled out a cigarette.

Stacy removed the cigarette from her cousin's fingers and handed it back to her. They had discussed the no-smoking policy repeatedly. There wouldn't be any compromise. Sabrina could roll her eyes all she wanted, it wasn't happening.

"I want to hear what he does for a living. Where he's from. Doesn't sound like he's from around here. His accent is from up North."

"Maryland. He's got a family, brother and sisters. He's the white-house-with-picket-fence sort."

"Whoa! He looks too hip for that. And the boy next door is too tame for you. He'll bore you in a second."

"He's finding his own rhythm here in Atlanta.

Maybe I'm in the mood for a change." Stacy knew she'd been skirting the same thought. Talking about her feelings gave her more confidence.

"I think I'll need a second cup. Kids, go play in your auntie's room. Mommy's not done talking." Fran and Lenny disappeared.

"I'll keep them company." Omar stepped into the kitchen, accepted the cup of coffee from Stacy, winked and left.

"What nonsense are you saying? The music was supposed to get you out of the neighborhood, change your lifestyle, give you some bling," Sabrina lectured.

"I *am* out of the neighborhood, in case you haven't noticed. The bling is overrated."

"Brenda must be going ballistic over the new you. Is that why you're back here in Atlanta? I figured you'd be in Hollywood or New York. You haven't been this quiet and low-key, ever."

At the mention of Brenda, Stacy started looking for her cell phone. She moved around the kitchen, lifting up mail, moving dishes to locate her lifeline. Having slept on the issue with Brenda, she knew that she'd acted impulsively. Her feelings hadn't changed, but she should have done a better job convincing Brenda. She'd let her dictate her behavior.

"What's the problem?" Sabrina started looking around the kitchen, copying Stacy's motions.

"My cell phone. Maybe Brenda called."

"If you dropped that mess on her like you did with me, then yep, she'll be calling you to see if you'd stop sniffing glue."

Stacy headed for her pocketbook and pulled out the phone. Still no call.

Stacy didn't want to seem rude, but she hurriedly hugged her cousin and then had Omar escort her and the children to the car with their fresh laundry and toys. She took the few minutes that she was alone to call Brenda.

The phone rang. Stacy bit her lip, hoping that Brenda would pick up. Any moment, she expected the voice mail to kick in.

"Yes."

"Brenda, it's Stacy."

"Yes, Stacy," Brenda said in a monotone.

"Do you have any free time this afternoon? I wanted to talk," Stacy requested.

"Don't think so."

"Oh." Stacy didn't count on that. Brenda was always available to her, any time of the day, any day of the week. "I wanted to talk about the other day," Stacy further explained.

"I bet you do. But you can come by the office on Monday."

Stacy could hear Omar's return. She couldn't possibly hang up while her relationship with

Brenda hung on such a thin thread. "Brenda, don't do this to me. I'm sorry for saying what I did. You deserve more respect than that." Omar was almost at her door.

"Come over at three."

"Thanks, Brenda. Bye."

Brenda hung up on her without another word. Stacy set her phone down and worked to put on a relaxed, happy face.

"That Sabrina can talk your ear off." Omar walked to the window and looked down. "I felt like pulling up a couch so she could play talk-show host. She was all up in my stuff."

"That's my cousin. Better you than me." She walked up behind him and placed her head against his back. "I enjoyed waking up in your arms."

"I enjoyed it, too." He turned to face her, and lifted her chin with his finger. "Where do we go from here?"

"Now, that's the multimillion-dollar question. If I said that I wanted you every day and night, when I wake up and before I go to sleep, you'd think I had only lust in my heart. But if I said that I'd like to take things slowly, I'm not in the market for a relationship, then it would sound like I'm giving you the brush-off." The problem was that a part of her belonged in both camps.

"I'd say that you worry too much about what

other people think." He placed his fingertips against her lips, preventing her from speaking. "Don't say anything. The next time that we discuss our future will be from your heart. I know what I want. I can see the indecision in your eyes." He shook his head as she rose to defend herself. "It's okay. I'm not going anywhere. I'm too busy trying to climb the corporate ladder," he joked.

Stacy gripped his shirt collar and sank her face into his throat. His pulse beat a steady rhythm against her forehead. Though she had a racing heartbeat and a nervous edge, he appeared unruffled. His muscled arms locked her against his body. His voice was like a cool hand on a hot day, providing a soothing comfort.

"I think you're a keeper," Stacy groaned.

Omar headed to work. It was Saturday, and he had nothing better to do than to go to work. But he wouldn't let his idea die. Access to the various databases he needed could only happen at work. Maybe while he was knee deep with work, he'd stop thinking about Stacy. She had opened a door for him that unfettered some of the self-doubts that crippled his abilities. He might have gotten only a glimpse of what lay beyond the door, but now he recognized his potential.

A few workaholics who had their own causes

were already in the building. Omar greeted them and headed to his work area. After settling in and logging on to his computer, he checked his e-mail. His piece on Stacy in Montreal had not aired yet. There were more delays than he liked, but the movie studio people were being a pain because they didn't want her preempting their stars or marketing pitch.

He had gone in to the editing session and could vouch that anything related to the movie had been taken out. On his end, the company president had created a firestorm that another studio dared tell him what to do. So much for all the preplanning and logistical meetings to land the interview with Stacy. Plus there was Brenda, who played the unhappy manager to the hilt. She didn't care for some of Stacy's responses or how he'd edited them. Part of the interview was to highlight Stacy's transition to movies.

Omar wasn't holding his breath that the piece would actually air. He pulled up a search engine on the Internet and typed in *Stacy Watts*. The results produced information that he already knew. Photos of her in glitz and glamour stared back at him. She was a gorgeous woman with hair and makeup to rival any fashion photographer's work. Yet he admired her in their private time, with little to no makeup, allowing her natural beauty to shine through with equal strength.

"I'm like a teen with a big crush," he muttered. He was moving the cursor on the computer monitor to close the window when he saw a link to a newspaper article with a short description of Antonio Perez. Antonio—the only reason that Stacy was interested in him.

He clicked on the link and pulled his chair forward to review the article. Antonio had gone ahead with his press conference. What was clear, however, was no one was interested, except for this small newspaper. Omar finished the article, shaking his head. He might not know every fact about Stacy, but he could sense that Antonio had blown things way out of proportion, trying to boost his role in Stacy's life to demigod status.

Omar printed the article to share it with Stacy. He didn't think that she or Brenda had caught wind of this in the press. Once more, he read the article. Now he focused on a couple of lines about Stacy. She had been living on the streets. She had come from a community of homeless kids in the Miami Beach area. She had been associated with a street gang.

Stacy didn't owe him an explanation. But they were behaving like a couple and couples talk and share their lives. He had never once cast judgment on her. He knew that Antonio was a threat to a past that she distanced herself from.

Omar picked up the phone and dialed. Stacy answered.

"Hey." His voice softened to match her husky whisper. "Were you sleeping?"

"No." There was a pause. "I'm at Brenda's. We had some things to take care of."

"Well, that's great because I have something that both of you need to know. Can we meet?"

"Can we do it during the week?"

"Hey, are you okay?" It sounded as if she was crying. He distinctively heard her sniffing.

"Yeah." She inhaled and sighed wearily.

"It's about Antonio," Omar said.

"Antonio. My Antonio?"

Omar tightened his grip on the phone. Jealousy had never been a weakness for him. But no one had captured his heart, either. The unfamiliar, sharp jab poked him unmercifully.

"Omar? You still there?"

Omar nodded, then, remembering that he was on the phone, answered, "Yes."

"Wait a sec." He heard her talking to someone in the background. "Hey. Brenda said to come on over."

Omar got the address and hung up. Yes, he was going over to see Stacy and Brenda, but she hadn't made it easy for him. Instead of having a meeting where they could all sit and plan how to handle this development, he felt very much the outsider.

Feeling sick to his stomach, he drove across the city to Alpharetta, Brenda's home. Most of the article had been committed to his memory. On the drive, parts of Antonio's testimony replayed in his mind. The man's seediness nestled in Omar's mind and burned with the fuel of his anger. He pulled up to the gated community, identified himself and drove through once the guard received approval.

Omar noticed the massive mansions, but he was too focused to enjoy or envy. He pulled up to a driveway lined with evergreens snaking up to a large three-story English-manor-style home.

The front door opened while he parked and Stacy stepped out. She didn't run up to the car, didn't wave at him with any excitement, didn't have the warm, lustful expression that she'd had only hours ago. Did his news, especially about Antonio, mute any feelings she had for him? He grabbed the article and got out of the car.

"Hi, Stacy," he said, embarrassed at his own hesitation.

"Brenda's waiting." She offered a smile that one would offer as a polite acknowledgment to a stranger.

Omar hurried to catch up with her. She'd turned

and headed back into the house. Her subdued attitude worried him. He attempted a weak joke. "Can we chat before we go into Medusa's home?"

"You shouldn't make fun of Brenda," Stacy scolded.

Omar raised his hand in a semiapologetic gesture. Although he'd planned to include Brenda in the news, he didn't take it for granted that he had moved off her least favorite list.

Their footsteps echoed against the dark wood floors. The decorations in the house were dark and ornate as if stuck in centuries past. The furniture and surroundings didn't fit the Georgian style, nor its owner. He wondered if Brenda could possibly be house-sitting.

Stacy never slowed her step for him to walk beside her. She kept the physical distance between them. He resisted pushing this point, since she obviously didn't want to talk.

Omar entered what he figured was a formal sitting room. Brenda sat in one of the chairs, with legs crossed, her body erect, expression stoic. He expected to see royal lackeys on each side of the chair as he approached.

"Have a seat, Omar." So much for "Hi and how are you?"

Omar followed the command, looking over at Stacy. She sat in a chair similar to Brenda's. The chair also made her look stiff and uptight. Her expression solidified the look.

"What do you have for us?" Brenda stared at him.

Omar handed over copies to Brenda and Stacy. He noticed that Stacy's hand shook and she played with her lower lip. No matter how hard he tried, she wouldn't look up into his face. She had shut herself off from him.

He didn't take his eyes off her as she lowered her head to read the article. Her body jerked, reacting to the content.

"I'm going to nail this bastard to the wall," Brenda declared, a thick vein protruding along her neck. "Let me call Marty."

Stacy popped out of the chair and ran out of the room. Omar didn't wait to see what Brenda's reaction was. He followed Stacy and saw her hurry down the hall before disappearing in a room on the right.

"Stacy?" He stood outside the door.

She ignored him, but had her cell phone to her ear. Omar could only wait until she'd completed the call. He moved slowly into the room, approaching her with certain deliberation, as if he expected her to take flight.

"Antonio, I want a meeting. Now. I'll come to Miami." She paused, her hand covering her mouth. "You're here? Okay."

Omar stopped in midstride.

She snapped the phone closed, grabbed her pocketbook and swept past him. His arm shot out and grabbed hers. Although she resisted, he didn't release her.

"Talk to me," he pleaded.

"I can't," her reply erupted like a cry. "You can't fix this." She shook her head as if having an argument with herself. "I don't want you to fix this. Just give me space." She held her head and the tears coursed down her face.

Omar didn't wait another second, but pulled her to him. "Whatever you want to do, we'll do it together."

"No. My past is too ugly. I couldn't bear for you to see any part of it," she uttered, her words filled with sobbing hiccups. She pushed away and headed out the door. "I have to get to a meeting."

"Fine." Omar followed her down the hallway.

As she approached the door, she looked over her shoulder. "Are you going to follow me?"

"If you don't let me come with you, then yes." Omar heard Brenda join them and stepped aside. He didn't want an argument, but neither woman would deter him. Stacy was not going to meet with Antonio on her own.

"I'll drive." Brenda stepped between them and walked out the door.

Stacy uttered a frustrated groan, but followed. Omar walked quickly to keep up with them.

"Where are you meeting him? I certainly hope it's not in a dump." Brenda sped through the traffic like a professional driver. Traffic lights did little to slow her down. Pedestrians didn't realize how close they came to serious injury as she honked and sped around stragglers on the crosswalk.

"Since I didn't plan on meeting him, I had to go with his meeting place. I also wasn't planning on having an entourage," Stacy added sullenly.

"You don't have a clue how that maniac will react. And you're no bigger than a little bit. Come off the tough-girl routine," Brenda scolded.

Omar, for once, agreed with Brenda. For his sake, though, he wished that she wasn't there. He didn't want to feel censored when he went full-throttle with this man.

"May I ask what's the game plan?" He directed his question to Stacy.

"There is no plan. I want to know why he won't leave me alone. Why he has set his mind to ruining me. How can I get him off my back?"

"I don't think you need to meet with him to get those answers." Omar sat behind Brenda. He looked between the seats at Stacy's profile. She refused to face him. "He seems to have a problem letting go."

Stacy turned her face to the window. He couldn't tell if she was blocking out what he had to say.

"I think that you should introduce me as your boyfriend," Omar offered.

"That's no longer necessary," Brenda replied, staring at him in the rearview mirror. "You're no longer needed. Antonio has already gone to the papers. Stacy is doing fine in the news without you."

Omar opened his mouth to deliver a blistering comeback. He waited, knowing that Stacy would set her straight. Instead Stacy remained silent, looking out the window.

"Don't bother looking at Stacy. She understands where her priorities need to be. She would have told you, but we weren't finished with our meeting when you called."

"What have I done to make you hate me so much?" Omar asked Brenda the question with all the honesty and bewilderment that he felt.

"No one hates you, Omar." Stacy finally turned to face him. Although his face was less than a foot away, she refused to look him in the eye. "I've been acting with no regard to my responsibility as an entertainer. I have missed wonderful opportunities because I'm consumed by you."

"Don't you sound like a robot? Brenda, this is your brainwashing technique at work."

"You amateurs always come into a celebrity's life with your average taste, average way of life, mediocre goals and force yourself into a lifestyle that is foreign to you. Count yourself lucky that you got to touch the brass ring, but now it's time for you to move on."

"Stop it, both of you!" Stacy placed her hands over her ears. "This isn't about you, Brenda, or you, Omar. I can't think. I don't want to think." She leaned her head against the window. "Let me get through this night."

"Look, we can have a press conference." Omar touched Stacy's shoulder. He wanted somehow to transfer his concern and reassurance to her body and take her pain and confusion.

"Absolutely not!" Brenda shouted. "We did that once and I don't think it's necessary to do it again. The media are like vultures ready to invade people's lives."

"Then you be the one to talk and be interviewed," Omar pressed on. He didn't like playing a docile role. He might be in the back seat, but he certainly wasn't planning to stay there in Stacy's life.

"No one is speaking to the media." Brenda glared at him in the mirror. "And that includes you." Her mouth tightened with such distaste that Omar felt it, like a physical wall keeping him in his place.

"I don't see what the problem is unless you've got something to hide," Omar stated.

Stacy turned and looked at him, long and hard. "Leave it alone. I don't want either of you coming in with me. This is between Antonio and me. I'm going to settle this matter tonight."

"Fat chance of that happening," Omar muttered before settling against the seat. He stared angrily out the window.

No one spoke. Each person concentrated on whatever issue had overtaken their thoughts. The business district, tall buildings and well-lit streets were left behind as they drove into a seedy residential area. As they turned down streets, they burrowed deeper into the community.

"It's the third house on the left." Stacy pointed to an older house with a large porch swing. Several individuals occupied the porch. They were casually dressed and lounging. Music blasted the neighborhood loud enough for a block party.

Brenda pulled up across the street. She turned off the engine, but didn't move. "If one of these fools messes with my car, it's on."

Omar stepped out and opened Stacy's door. She stared across the street at the house. The only movement on her face was the occasional blink of her eyes.

"I'm right next to you." Omar leaned forward

and offered his hand. She placed her small hand in his. It felt as if she had held on to a block of ice before they got there. He immediately placed his arm around her shoulders. "Don't worry. We're a team, remember." She nodded and stepped closer to his body, but her focus remained on the house.

Stacy was grateful for Omar's stubbornness. Despite her attempts to keep him away, she couldn't imagine walking into this house on her own. Already her breath fought to get through her throat. More than a frog was in her throat and more than a cat had her tongue. She had the shakes, and they started with her knees and traveled up her body. She gripped Omar's hand, hoping that her legs maintained momentum.

Like a five-star general, Brenda led this dismal parade. She practically marched through the gathering on the porch, her head held high. The people on the porch didn't stop talking to acknowledge the strangers, and Stacy and her group didn't offer any greetings as they ascended the stairs, maneuvered past the swing and paused in front of the open door.

A shirtless man with shorts hanging low on his hips stepped into their path. A thick beard covered the lower part of his tanned face, but his dark eyes glittered back with open animosity.

"We don't want any of your religion-toting garbage. And don't bother to say anything. I don't trust any of you not to put a curse on me." His thick West Indian accent would have enlightened any missionaries who stopped to visit about his feelings.

"Young man, we are here to meet with Antonio." Brenda stepped around the man, although he hadn't moved.

Stacy didn't move. Her feet remained glued to the ratty mat that was missing the letters *W* and *L* in *Welcome*. It was just as well. Nothing about the house or its owner could ever make her feel welcome.

Chapter 8

"Stanley, step aside. Let them through."

Stacy recognized that deep, raspy voice dulled by heavy cigarette use. Coldness crept over her body. Her feet moved, taking her closer to the man who had befriended, used and controlled her. She walked through the untidy living area, bypassing a mattress propped against a wall.

A musty odor permeated the room. Antonio could only exist in an environment where he fulfilled a leader's role. He would play the generous benefactor and have all sorts living on the premises.

"Come to me, Stacy."

Stacy followed the voice, but only the voice.

Ahead was another open room, which would have originally been the dining area. Its mood lights cast a pineapple-yellow color around the room. She stopped in the doorway, looking to find Antonio in the room and get a quick gauge of the situation.

"Looking better than ever." Antonio smiled.

Unlike his fellow residents, he was impeccably dressed in his favorite color—black. He leaned forward in the chair, but didn't stand. He still wore his hair low to the head, but now the sides were more peppered with gray. A die-hard vegetarian and health buff, he still looked taut and toned. His sleek dress style acted like a magnet for unwary souls, such as her.

"Ah, I see you are not alone." Antonio steepled his fingers under his chin. His eyes never left her face. But she knew that he was displeased to see Brenda and Omar.

"Antonio, we really need to talk and come to an agreement." Stacy's stomach churned and she was glad that she hadn't eaten anything for hours. Right now her heart pumped so hard she was afraid that the longer she talked, the more chance there was of her heart popping out of her chest.

He waved toward a sofa on his right. His gaze, however, fastened on Omar. "Introduce your new crewmates." Then his head snapped in her direction.

Stacy opened her mouth to make the necessary introductions.

"I'm Omar, Stacy's boyfriend, and this is Brenda, her manager."

Stacy's mouth snapped shut.

"You, I'll talk to later." Antonio pointed at Omar, but didn't offer him a seat. "And you, the wicked witch who came in like a vulture and swooped my baby girl out of my nest." His voice remained calm and restrained. "You, childless heathen, came onto my turf to find a new child to suckle on you."

"Antonio, stop, I'm asking you." Stacy closed her eyes, hoping that's all he said and all he could say.

Brenda brushed past Stacy to stand before Antonio. One hand was firmly planted on a hip and the other jabbed inches from Antonio's face. "Listen here, buster, you may sit there like the King of Pimps, but I'm not buying your crap. Stacy is a person, not a thing, not a possession, not one of those wannabe stars that you have dazzled sitting on your doorstep. If you were doing right by her, she would still be with you. I don't have to tell you what you lacked, because you don't have the good sense that God gave you to reflect on the empty shell of a man that you are."

The West Indian giant, Stanley, roared into the room, his eyes narrowed into slits with total focus on Brenda's back. Stacy jumped up and threw her body between Stanley and Brenda. She closed her eyes, steeling herself to absorb the physical blow.

Omar was quicker and pushed her back down. He performed a martial arts move with a throat chop that crumpled Stanley to the floor. The over-sized man fell to his knees holding his throat and wheezing. Antonio hadn't moved, but Stacy knew that the flare of his nostrils, the hooded look of his eyes, the working of his lips spelled pure rage.

"Are you going to give my girl the respect that she deserves or do I have to give you the same treatment?" Omar threatened.

Antonio blew out a breath. His hand uncurled and he rubbed his knees. A toothy grin appeared. "Glad to see that you didn't align yourself with a punk."

"Stop the name-calling, Antonio. I want to know why you won't leave me alone. You have moved on. I have moved on. Why do you torture yourself?" Stacy touched Brenda's arm and guided her to the sofa.

"I read all your interviews. I see you on the different talk shows. Not once do you give me any credit. You don't give me any credibility. And that makes me angry and sad." He slapped his heart.

"I'm sorry. But I'm trying to focus on my present and future."

"You weren't so ashamed of your past when I got you all the local gigs."

"But then I had to be your girl before that happened. It wasn't enough that you signed me to a contract that took everything. Am I supposed to be grateful? Am I supposed to say thank you, Antonio, for stomping over my self-worth? Brenda picked me up. She cared for me, sent me to school, taught me my business. I've built myself up." Stacy didn't mean to unveil her personal business to Antonio. She hadn't done that much for Omar.

"Stanley, stand up and be a man. Go put ice on that." Antonio waited until the man left the room. "Now he's a punk." He shook his head, disgust written all over his face. Then he crossed his legs and leaned back in the chair. "Omar, is that your name?"

Omar nodded.

"Let me tell you a thing or two about your girl-friend." Antonio's look dared Stacy to object.

She knew better than to try to stop him. He knew too much about her past, and that made him dangerous.

"Your little girl here had a mother with ques-tionable habits and a father who played musical beds with several women. Then he up and disappeared. Her mother wigged out on drugs and went on a journey. No one knows where, or they aren't saying. Then baby girl had to go live with her cousin. In a single-parent environment, she became one mouth too much to feed. She ended up in the foster-care system by the time she was twelve." He looked at her. "Am I right so far? Wouldn't want to give the wrong facts and screw up your man's perception of you.

"Two years later, she got bounced to another family. The foster parents were only interested in the money. They had strict rules for the foster children and corporal punishment for any offenders. She lived under threats that, if she told the social worker, they would never find her body. I met her where I hung out during the day at the boys' and girls' club. She'd come there for a break. One day a family friend came over to the house and got drunk. By the end of the night, he was making sexual advances toward her. She clocked him in the eye and ran. She ran to me."

Stacy grimaced.

"I got her in a shelter, but you can only stay there for a short while before they have to let your guardians know. But she wouldn't have survived on the street. Sometimes we were outside with no place to stay. I knew the street kids were a tough

bunch with limited options and a dismal future. I
didn't want that for her." Antonio's eyes shone
with a zeal that showed him obviously stuck in the
past. Stacy shuddered at his retelling of their
shared history.

"I worked to get her out there. Get the people
to know Stacy Watts. I sacrificed everything to
make her who she is now."

"Antonio, maybe I couldn't have got my career
started without you, but you couldn't get what
you had without me. I do believe that if this was
my destiny, it would have happened anyway."
Stacy took a deep, stabilizing breath. Saying the
thought that was in her head gave her strength. She
had a future. She didn't need to feel guilty or
scared of Antonio. His clothing, his mannerisms,
his thought processes were products of the past.
Now she saw him as a pathetic creature who
reacted out of fear—fear of her success.

Stacy looked over to Brenda and Omar. "These
are the people in my life now. These are the people
who will protect me and who have my best interests at heart. It's over. I don't want anything to do
with you. And you no longer can threaten me with
my past." Stacy turned to Brenda. "I'm ready to
go."

Stacy touched Omar's arm, encouraging him to
leave. Antonio, who had seemed larger than life,

now sat in his make-believe empire on a worn armchair in a house that he probably didn't own.

"I'm sorry for you," she said with a small wave.

"Don't you dare pity me." Antonio shot out of the chair. Omar stiffened, but placed a hand around Stacy's waist as they continued out. Stanley remained in the background, not giving any of them eye contact. "Since you claim that these people have your back, let's hope you have theirs. Omar? When you least expect it, you'll feel a sharp stab in your back and in your heart. It won't be a mystery who is the cause of that crime."

Omar tightened his arm around Stacy's waist. She walked out into the dusky night. Her chest hurt, aching for a breath of fresh air. People still lingered, uninterested in them. They headed for Brenda's car, lost in their own thoughts.

Stacy slid into the front seat without looking at Omar. Despite her tough words, she was afraid to face Omar's judgment, especially with Antonio's parting shot about injuring him.

"Stacy, you made me proud." Brenda reached over and patted her hand. "Let's move on. Let's look at this as closing the curtains."

Stacy nodded. Exhaustion flooded her. She couldn't wait for Brenda to get to the house so she could head home. The day had been long and emotional. What she craved now was quiet.

As soon as Brenda parked, Stacy hopped out of the car. She ran toward hers, hoping Brenda and Omar would understand that she was not up for a prolonged analysis of the evening. After spending time with Antonio and being reminded of the hellish life she'd had to live, she now craved her home. It was more than shelter or refuge. Her home allowed her to regenerate and regain whatever life had taken from her.

"Call me when you're ready," Brenda called from her doorway. Stacy heard her, but didn't respond. Her goal was to hop in her car and get home. An overwhelming need to cry grew more powerful and threatened to break.

"Stacy," Omar called, drawing her attention to the driveway. She looked over the top of the car to where he stood. For the first time that night, she looked at him without avoiding his eyes. Omar didn't deserve to be compared to Antonio, for there was nothing comparable.

His legs were slightly apart, hands dangling at his sides, his face partly shadowed by the lengthening darkness of the night. She didn't need a protector. She didn't need a guardian. She didn't need a man to run her life. Omar would fill any of those roles, if she let him.

"Don't run," he said.

"I've always been running." Then the hot tears

surfaced and she bit her cheek to shut that emotional pain off. "Let me run one more time." She got into the car and started the engine. She wanted to drown out anything else he had to say. Her willpower couldn't hold up against anything that he wanted from her. But she didn't want to be with him as a way to escape the pain.

She sobbed openly as she drove out of Brenda's neighborhood. Grabbing a tissue, she wiped away the tears as quickly as they came. Her breath hitched and her nose ran. All she wanted was a quiet oasis to settle old demons that tortured her conscience.

As much as spending the night in Omar's arms appealed to her, she couldn't do it. He didn't deserve to be used as a pacifier. Her cell phone rang. Omar's number flashed on the tiny window. She ignored the persistent ringing. Once it went to voice mail, she turned off the phone. It was times like this that she wished she had a brother or sister to confide in or a mother who could hold her hand and tell her that everything would be all right.

Sabrina, her cousin, didn't fit that bill. Her cousin could pretend that their childhood was normal. But Stacy could vividly remember the nights of eating crackers soaked in milk and sugar as the dinner meal.

In her condo, she dropped her keys on the counter. Then she walked into the bathroom and filled the tub with painfully hot water. She didn't plan to get out anytime soon and needed the water to stay comfortable for as long as possible. With the right amount of bath oil, bath beads and other concoctions, she allowed the water to fill. She debated on a glass of wine, but changed her mind. Alcohol and her mood didn't mix.

Her home phone rang. She paused in disrobing. Omar's voice played over the speaker.

"Stacy, I'm worried about you. Don't ride through this alone. I may not have lived the life that you did, but I do know a thing or two about running from who you are or were. You don't have to talk if you don't want to. I can just be there with no demands, no obligations."

Stacy walked nude into the bathroom. "I'm sorry, Omar," she said to the small space. She lowered herself into the tub, wincing at the heat. "I don't think you can be with me without demanding a commitment eventually." She leaned back her head with her eyes closed. "Everyone wants a commitment."

Omar waited in the lobby of Stacy's condo, hoping that she would relent. Regardless of his deep feelings for her, he recognized that she had dealt with a lot of emotional baggage for a long time. His own inadequacies frustrated him. Yet he was sure that he should be there with her. He snapped closed his cell phone, tapping it against his head for inspiration on how to reach Stacy, then opened it again.

"Hi, Brenda, could you do me a favor?" Omar explained what he needed. He trusted that their mutual experience earlier that day had melted some of the ice around their relationship.

Then he dialed another person whom he hoped was an ally. "Hi, Sabrina, could you do me a favor?"

Omar sat in the chair opposite the elevator doors, praying for success. Less than thirty minutes later, the doors opened. He stifled a yawn and looked up. Most would have given up and gone home.

"Omar Masterson, you are a real pain." Stacy stood her ground near the elevator, glaring at him.

Omar didn't wait to exchange any words. He didn't trust her not to head back up to her condo alone. Instead, he gently guided her into the elevator, asking, "Are you going to press the button?"

"Oh, shut up," she said crossly.

"Your sweatsuit is becoming."

"No, it's not and don't try to sweet-talk me. I'm trying to have a quiet moment alone. Do you know what *alone* means? Then you call, then Brenda and the final pain was Sabrina. I can't believe that you got them to play your silly game."

Omar accepted her irritation. It didn't matter. He was heading up to her condo with her. He had imagined all kinds of sordid things about her mental state and what she might be up to. From her feisty demeanor, he needn't have worried.

"You're not staying." Stacy poked him in the chest.

Omar followed her into the condo.

"Water?" She opened her refrigerator, which was dismally empty.

"How do you survive?"

"I order in. I also have my groceries delivered. I'll get them tomorrow."

"You don't even have milk? So when you had the kids over, did you buy it specially for that occasion?"

Stacy nodded. "You're beginning to annoy me." She walked past him and headed toward her bedroom. "Why are you so insistent on seeing me? Tonight?" She spoke through the closed bedroom door.

"I'm sorry. Thought you might need a friend."

"Sure. You got any ideas who?"

Omar stopped in his pacing to stare at the closed door. Then he broke into a grin. "Nice one. I see you got back your sense of humor."

Stacy emerged from the room wearing a long cotton nightdress. The oversized shape muted hers, but he didn't need a visual to know what was under the designs of moons and stars. A frill at the bottom had a peekaboo effect with her manicured toes. All in all, she looked sexy.

"Don't give me that look. I'm tired and I want to go to bed." Stacy pulled her hair into a ponytail. The effect was to highlight the beauty of her face. "I allowed you to come in because you ganged up on me and I wanted a little peace."

"I hear you and understand. I only want to sleep with you." Omar walked toward her and gathered her up in his arms. He pushed the bedroom door wider with his foot and carried her into the room.

"Omar, what do you think you're doing?" Stacy protested, with her arms laced around his neck.

The fresh, clean scent from her body made him think of an open prairie scented with wildflowers. She nuzzled his neck and he came dangerously close to breaking his own plan. Her cotton nightdress reminded him of his mother, but his arms holding her body, with only the thin material between her skin and his hands, fueled all sorts of images.

He eased her into the bed. With deliberate action, he pulled the comforter over her body and then tucked it in on the side. He kissed her forehead and turned off the lamp near her head. "Sweet dreams."

She looked perplexed, but didn't speak. He walked to the other side of the bed and pulled off his shirt.

"What are you doing?" Stacy sat upright in the bed.

Omar continued taking his shoes and socks off. Then he pulled off his pants. In his boxers, he offered an apologetic smile. "Didn't mean to disturb you. I'm getting into bed now, not to worry." He leaned up and turned off the bedside lamp.

"Do you think you are so darn charming that you can force me to have a wild night with you?"

"Of course not. I told you that I wanted to sleep with you. Here, let me put the pillow right here." He pulled the pillow close to his arm. "Okay, I'll let you snuggle until we fall asleep."

"You're serious." Stacy's incredulity amused him.

He nodded. "Now stop talking, so I can get some sleep." He scooted his body next to hers and snuggled the back of her neck. If she only knew how much he had to concentrate not to act on his arousal.

On Monday, Omar had no problem getting to work on time. He'd barely slept, what with Stacy breathing heavily in her sleep and her butt pressed into his pelvis. But he wanted her to feel safe and to know that he could exhibit restraint.

One of his colleagues poked his head into his office. "Staff meeting in five minutes."

He hated being kept in the dark. His planner didn't reflect any staff meetings. He was supposed to meet with the head of publicity this morning. His plan was to work on each stakeholder who would have a say in his plans for a new documentary.

Since this meeting was impromptu, this was a sign that his boss would be in a foul mood. Something must have happened that couldn't be handled individually. More than likely, his boss wanted to make an example out of another person.

"Let's go," another colleague urged.

By the time they had arrived at the conference room, there was a small traffic jam as they all herded through the doorway. His boss was already in place, scrutinizing each attendee and making notes on a writing pad.

"Let's get started. I brought you all together to hear of a new idea that will be added to the lineup in early spring. Mr. Baxter will join us. It's an honor to have the CEO and president sit in on our project from the ground up. Miss Rosa Sanchez, take it away."

A statuesque Latina with olive-toned skin, sleek black hair and professionally made-up features stood. All the men gasped and the women self-consciously checked themselves. Rosa was a recent hire, apparently. Little to no information was revealed prior to her arrival. Wherever she came from, she commanded each person's attention. Maybe she was Miss World and the production company wanted to capitalize on her fame.

"Hi, I'm Rosa. I'm so happy to be here, joining the team. I am especially glad to be given the opportunity to start a documentary series where I will focus on the problems in the Latino teen community and bring them to the people who watch our shows. Mr. Baxter and Mr. Henderson are the inspiration for this vision." She clapped her hands and everyone followed suit. "I think that this will really open up the diversity of our viewing audience." She smiled toward the staff and resumed her seat.

Stunned, Omar had to force his mouth closed. While everyone chatted excitedly about the new show, he had difficulty focusing on anything. The room seemed too bright. The chatter seemed too loud. The temperature seemed too warm.

"You lucky devil, you'll be working with that hot new chick," one of his male coworkers said, openly gawking at Rosa.

"What?" Omar asked, feeling as though his brain had been replaced with thick cotton balls.

"Mr. Henderson announced that she will piggyback on your show for the documentary specials. Gosh, I envy you, man." His colleague slapped him on the shoulder, a deep chuckle rumbling through his large frame.

Then all of Omar's senses collided, along with the reality. His feelings, his reaction, everyone's jubilation and his boss's betrayal roared back at him like a punch to the gut. He leaned back in his chair to absorb the impact, its sting, to catch his breath.

"You're looking sick," Henderson announced, approaching him with a frown. "Hope you're not catching something." He stopped a few feet away.

Omar bit back a caustic reply. Instead, he responded, "I'd like to talk to you."

"Sure. After the meeting, stop by my office." Henderson grinned. In that instant, Omar knew that this episode was no mistake. He had been given the shaft.

Omar couldn't wait for the meeting to be over. He didn't hear anything else that was said. He replayed all the various ways he would go into his boss's office and tell him where to shove his job.

Finally the meeting ended. While his coworkers offered congratulations to Rosa, Omar chose to leave the room. He had to get his anger in check. Knowing how tenuous holding his temper would be, he grabbed his cell phone and headed out of the building.

"Hey, Pierce."

"Omar? What's happening? Haven't talked to you in a while, little brother."

"It's been crazy busy over here. Got a sec?"

"Not really. You caught me between patients. You don't sound good."

Suddenly Omar felt stupid calling his big brother for help. He was a man with a good job. Calling Pierce would make him look weak in his brother's eyes. Although Pierce would be good with doling out the right way to handle this situation, Omar had to learn to do this on his own. "Go back to your patients. I'll be fine."

"I don't believe you, but I do have to run. Omar, come home for a visit. Everyone misses you. I miss you, man."

"Sure. Talk to you later." Omar ended the call without a game plan, but he felt more clearheaded after talking to his brother. Pierce must be getting old or fatherhood had softened him quite a bit. They had been on the opposite sides of the spectrum. Pierce had played emotionally removed leader, dictator and big brother. While Omar and his siblings had fallen apart after their mother died and their father had already left, Pierce had steered their ship to safe harbor.

Meanwhile Omar had been the quick-tempered, impulsive character who lived up to all the stereotypes of being the youngest. His anger over the loss of his parents, his rebellious nature, conflicted with the others. He took classes in college that he knew would irritate Pierce. Then, when the family got on his case about a career, he promised to do law to show Pierce that he could be equally as successful in a stable career as he was. Even then he had failed because it was not what he really wanted to do.

He looked up at the large building that was his current place of employment. Here he had thought he had a future. Stacy had waded past his arrogant pickup lines and lover-boy ploys to recommend a job that suited his personality.

In front of the camera, talking with kids and interviewing celebrities, he enjoyed the interactive nature of the job. He'd planned to work hard, impress the powers-that-be and contribute to the success of their programming.

Now he felt as if someone had kicked him in the teeth. His idea that had drawn excitement from the president and been dismissed by his boss had been plucked from him. With no plan in mind, he walked back into the building. At the very least, he wanted to hear what Henderson had to say.

"Omar, good, you're here. I wondered where you had run off to."

Omar entered the room that no longer held him in awe. As far as he was concerned, the office had the personality of its owner—cold, dark and unwelcoming.

Henderson pushed a button on his phone console. "Felicia, send in Rosa."

"I wanted to talk to you in private."

"Go ahead, but make it quick. I want you and Rosa to start bouncing off ideas."

"I'm really not understanding what is happening. I came to you with an idea. An idea that you thought I couldn't do. Yet I get blindsided at that meeting with someone who probably doesn't have any credentials, now doing my idea," Omar roared.

"Noted. You had an idea. And it's great ideas that will keep you employed in this competitive industry. However, ideas don't bring in the ratings. We need someone that the kids can relate to and trust."

"I have that now."

"Yes, but we are not focusing on a niche. You've got the hip-hop generation, but we are going global. We want to hit all kids, regardless of whether they listen to rap. Our demographics have changed. We need to keep up with the times."

Chapter 9

Rosa Sanchez entered the office, providing her new boss with a dazzling white smile. She offered Omar her hand, which he dutifully shook. The air of conflict had lit the room with volatile tension. Omar stared at the antique desk separating his boss from him in an effort to keep his feelings from being revealed on his face.

"Rosa, Omar has some great ideas for this show. I would like to see you work together so we can get the ball rolling. Any questions?"

Rosa shook her head. Omar didn't respond.

"Good. You can use my conference room to

meet." Henderson indicated a door off to the side of his office.

"We wouldn't want to put you out," Omar said with dripping sarcasm.

"Wouldn't hear of it. Besides, I might want to look in on both of you to see how you're doing."

Omar read the open threat. Now that he'd officially revealed himself as a rebel, he would be watched. Conform or be fired.

He headed for the conference room, knowing that he had to give an illusion of cooperating.

"Rosa, tell me about yourself," Omar directed.

"I worked with Miami Univision as an assistant editor. Then I heard through the grapevine that UTP was looking for a person fluent in Spanish to host a new show for the burgeoning Latino market. I showed up and auditioned."

Omar provided his background, not because she asked, but because he felt obligated. This woman had come into the middle of a situation and was completely unaware that she was a pawn in corporate politics.

"So where do we start?" Rosa asked.

"Figured you would be asking me that." Omar wasn't going out of his way to ease her transition.

"I just started." Rosa laughed. "I haven't even signed my paperwork with Human Resources. I need a little help."

"Well, this is what I'm going to do for you." Omar stood. He opened the conference room door and walked into his boss's office without knocking. "I have to leave to conduct interviews. Rosa needs an orientation. She's not sure what she's supposed to be doing. I'll pick up where you leave off when I return." He walked out of Henderson's office, not bothering to wait for a reply.

He walked over to his work area, picked up his jacket, threw it over his arm and headed for the elevators. There comes a time when you measure how much you have to lose. He had a vision that had ignited his passion and that had great possibility. Maybe this place was only a stepping stone, but he would not let them trample and dilute what he wanted to do.

Omar set off to conduct his interviews. The young celebrities had learned to trust him and his instincts. Unlike most reporters who only wanted to highlight controversies, Omar brushed that aside to find the inner workings and influences of his young stars; sometimes revealing their human frailties could help young audience members with their problems.

His growing list of celebrity friends could also help him pursue his dream. His pride could have gotten him in trouble, but he was willing to take the chance. Nothing came easy. Henderson didn't know that he'd have to deal with the Masterson tenacity.

His phone rang. "Hi, Pierce. I was just thinking about you."

"Hey, little brother, you didn't sound good earlier. I wanted to make sure that I caught up with you before I headed home. Talk to me."

Omar didn't hesitate to update Pierce. He detailed from landing the job up to the present. He parked at the country club where he would conduct his interview. Since he was twenty minutes early, he continued chatting with Pierce.

"What do you need from me?" Pierce asked, after Omar finished talking to him.

"I was calling for advice."

"It's too late for my input. You've taken some decisive actions."

"Guess it is." Omar exhaled, and rubbed his hand over his tensed face.

"Or it could be that I don't have any advice to give you. I think, little brother, that you have graduated."

"What are you talking about?"

"Sounds like you handled things the way you should have."

"Whoa! This is a moment." Omar laughed along with his brother. "Remind me to say thank-you to Haley for making you a lovable teddy bear."

"You do and I'll have to give you the death grip."

Omar remembered how much he and his older brother had fought as kids, a constant irritant to each other. Then all of that had changed when they'd lost their parents. His brother had gone through a rapid metamorphosis from child to adult, raising his younger siblings. All Omar's anger at missing out on what his older siblings had enjoyed with their parents had simmered. His brother could say that the sky was blue and he'd argue and fight him that the sky was red as a way to rebel.

Leaving his hometown in Maryland and his sister's home in Atlanta, he had finally struck out on his own. With his job, and with Stacy now a part of his life, he believed that he'd grown up.

"I've listened to what you have planned and it sounds fantastic. I'll support you in whatever way you need," Pierce said.

"Thanks, bro. That means a lot."

"Look, I'm serious. Why don't you come down for a long weekend? And why don't you bring that girl you told me you are seeing. You know your big sis would want to meet her."

"Sheena will give her hell. I remember how she treated Haley."

"And now they are best friends, a bit too much bonding, if you ask me. I'm outnumbered." Pierce laughed.

"Okay, let me see what I can do, especially with Stacy's busy schedule." Omar looked at his watch. "Gotta run." He hung up.

Now his mood soared. He had an hour ahead of him that promised to be fun and informative. Then he'd return to work and survey the damage. Now that his emotions had settled, he also knew that he owed Rosa an apology. He might not be happy that she had come on board to take charge of his idea, but it was not her fault. However, he didn't plan to give up on his version of the documentary.

Stacy had awakened fully rested in Omar's arms. He was already awake, looking down at her. She snuggled closer, enjoying the warmth emanating from his body. It had been so long since she'd experienced such calmness, and this was the first time that she'd fallen in love. And what a glorious fall it was.

"Are we going to stay in this position all day?" Stacy asked, stretching her arms and legs.

"I've got to get to work, but we can continue later today."

"Promise?" She kissed the tip of his nose.

"Pinky swear." They performed the childhood ritual for promises.

"I'm dying to make love to you." Stacy took his hand and slid it over her breast.

"The feeling is mutual, but I promised that we would only sleep together. Consider it a quick abstinence. The next time we make love, I'm calling the shots."

"That's fine." Stacy smirked at him. He was just wrong, making her feel like this.

"On that note, I have to go to work." He slid out of the bed and retrieved his clothes. "Got to head home and get cleaned up. Yesterday was unplanned on lots of levels."

Stacy groaned, not happy with the coldness that invaded her space when Omar stood up. She hugged her pillow and watched him dress. "Are you eating breakfast?"

Omar shook his head. "I'll grab a cup of coffee on the way in." As he buttoned his shirt, he looked down at her. "What's the plan for your day?"

Stacy shrugged. She didn't want to think about what she had to do. She had reconciled differences with Brenda. Her impromptu meeting with Antonio made her rethink what she wanted to do. She wanted to talk to Brenda before anyone else.

"Call if you need me." Omar kissed her mouth, gave her nose a playful tap and left.

Her phone rang. Omar took the cue to leave. Stacy answered the phone, still thinking about Omar.

"Good morning, Stacy, it's Brenda. We need to

get started with everything early. I need you to come over soon. I've got appointments lined up all day."

"Sure." Stacy cut the telephone conversation short. She had some major issues to discuss. She wasn't about to lay down an ultimatum with Brenda, but she had to be on board.

Stacy deliberated over her wardrobe and selected a trim black-and-white fitted suit. She brushed her hair into a ponytail with a flip on the end. Although she preferred to go without makeup, she added a little eye color and foundation to hide any imperfections. Her neutral colors enhanced her mixture of Native-American and African-American features.

An hour later, Stacy sat in Brenda's office. Brenda was the image of cool control. She had also chosen a black suit, but hadn't broken the monochromatic theme with another color. Her signature Afro hairstyle appeared to have been recently trimmed.

"You will head to the studio for the animation-picture audition," Brenda directed. "Then I'll need you to fly to New York because one of the directors wants to talk to you about a guest spot on an off-Broadway play. You'll come back tomorrow, then we have to start on the new album. There are several pieces that have been written for you."

In a snap, Stacy knew why this business held such a bittersweet feeling. She came alive onstage, pouring her heart out, sharing with her audience. Yet the behind-the-scenes absolutely drained her. She hated days that seemed to have no end because she flew through time zones and awoke before the sun broke through the horizon.

"Stacy, don't start pouting and blocking me out," Brenda warned. "Don't let Antonio mess with your head."

What she felt had nothing to do with Antonio. "I'm doing this because it will help fund what I want to do."

"And what is that?"

"Don't worry. It's nothing in the entertainment field. My own private venture that I'm feeling compelled to do."

Brenda frowned. "As long as it doesn't conflict."

"With your plans, never," Stacy finished.

"Don't be flip. I carry out your wishes." Brenda pushed away from her desk. "Why must you be difficult?"

"I'm really sorry. You know how much I hate to travel. And this schedule depresses me because I will be away from home and…"

"And what? I know you're not about to mention that man's name. Now you can't get rid of him."

Brenda shook her head. "I knew this would happen."

"I don't want to get rid of him." Stacy grabbed her coat and pocketbook. "I...like him." She dared not say any other word that would reflect a stronger feeling. This morning when she'd opened her eyes and he was there, she'd tested the thought in her head that she was in love. The unique feeling of being satisfied brought happiness.

"Have you met his family? Do you know how many girlfriends he's had? Do you know if he really likes you beyond the celebrity status?" Brenda fired the questions, brushing aside any attempts at her response.

Stacy headed for the door. Lately, she didn't like the way her conversations with Brenda deteriorated. The two of them used to be productive and supportive, a family of sorts. Omar had certainly driven a wedge between them, a catalyst for change.

"You know, Brenda, I'm not Valerie. I'm not rejecting you." Stacy paused to see if Brenda had heard her. Her manager's back was to her. Brenda's shoulders were stiff, with one hand cupping the side of her face.

Stacy opened the door and exited. She could never replace Valerie and had no intention of trying. But Brenda's attitude toward her grew increasingly constrictive. Stacy worried that maybe Brenda needed to talk to a professional to deal with her daughter's absence.

With a few hours to go before her appointment, she chose to go to one of her favorite hangouts to wait and eat until she had to go to the studio. On the way to the restaurant, she passed a small post office. She pulled out an envelope, hesitating for a brief second. Things had a way of spiraling out of control. But she'd started on a course and would have to deal with the consequences. If her plan didn't go the way she wanted, then how would she repair the damage? She dropped the letter in the domestic mail slot hoping that a resolution would come soon.

Stacy dined alone, a habit all too familiar. She opted for wonton soup and a chicken lo mein dish. When the mound of food arrived, she knew that there was no way she could eat the enormous serving.

She dialed Omar to tease him about her lunch. All she could do was exaggerate some details on the voice mail. A glance around the restaurant made her feel out of place. From the youngest to the oldest diner, they all had a dining partner. Normally she didn't mind eating alone. Since meeting Omar, she wanted to spend as much quality time as possible with him.

Her cell phone rang, disturbing the diners nearby. Stacy offered an apologetic smile and pushed the talk button. She'd risk dirty looks from strangers to talk to Omar.

"Got your message that you're heading out of town. That sucks that I won't see you this evening."

"This is how my life is when potential work is coming my way. Now that I'm focusing on more projects in the film world, I have to get in line with all the other starving actors."

"Well, if you need a character reference, I'm here for you," Omar teased.

"How was work today?"

"I think this is a conversation best had in person. Big stuff," Omar replied.

Stacy caught the immediate change in his voice. She set down her fork, giving him her full attention. "I can't go off to New York without knowing what happened." She looked at her watch. "I've got a small window of time after the audition before I have to head to the airport."

"I'm going back to the office right now. I may have time to take you to the airport," he said mysteriously.

"That would work. I'd like that," she encouraged. Whatever bombshell he was going to deliver couldn't wait. Besides, if he needed her help, she'd be happy to do whatever he needed. She provided him with the information for the flight. He arranged to pick her up from her condo.

Stacy finished her call, whispering seductive niceties to Omar. By the time she paid her bill, she had a wide smile on her face. Omar's threat of giving her a farewell quickie stirred her desire with prickly anticipation. She could only hope that the production team made a speedy decision, one way or the other, so that she could look forward to sharing precious time with Omar.

Stacy arrived at her appointment and walked through rows of hopeful actors to get to the woman signing everyone in. Stacy introduced herself, hoping that she had enough clout to get herself through the line quickly. If she didn't make it to New York tonight, she'd have to hop a plane early in the morning. Just what she needed, to have to face another audition after limited sleep and a harried flight.

"Miss Watts, glad you could make it. Follow me."

Surprised, Stacy hastened her steps to keep up with the petite woman scurrying through a series of rooms.

"Miss Watts, come on in." An older man beckoned to her.

Despite his age, his attire was trendy and fashionable. Like many celebrities he wore a pair of dark designer shades, although they were indoors. He embodied the role of man-in-charge and was wearing the most gaudy gold-and-diamond pinky ring.

"I'm Reynaldo Portee." He waved a hand and flashed a superwhite smile. "Everybody calls me Reynaldo."

He had an affected European accent and rolled his *R*s, but she couldn't pinpoint a specific country.

There were several other people in the room, busy at work in the background. Stacy didn't see any of the usual equipment. Was this a real audition? Or was she about to be caught up in a low-budget project that would harm her image?

"Have a seat, please." Stacy complied, sitting at a long table with the other people.

"There are specific voices that I want for this movie. Then we'll fly folks out to L.A. for work in the studios," Reynaldo explained. "Everyone, please introduce yourself to Stacy."

Stacy nodded to each person as they shared their names. She accepted a packet of material from a young man sitting next to her. "It's a sample of the script," he said.

"This is a story about an urban cat who breaks out of her gang and hides out in the suburbs. Then the leader of the gang gets help from the other gangs to come after her."

Stacy couldn't believe what she was hearing. Was this man for real? More importantly, what part of this project made Brenda think that this was a winning opportunity? "Let me guess, I'm supposed to be the urban cat?"

"No. We want you to be the leader of the skunk gang. You're fierce, arrogant but a little smelly." The others around the table chuckled.

"Let's try the lines," Reynaldo suggested.

Stacy waited for her turn to go into the other room for the audition. She wished she could hear their performances for tips on how she should perform. When it was her turn, she stepped into the room. Auditions made her stomach churn. She cleared her throat. "Yo, Renata, I'm going to have to go skunk-crazy and bash your head in."

"Whoa, stop." Reynaldo held up his hand. "Stacy, let's try that again. But I've got a few minor suggestions. I need you to use your inner-city attitude. When you say, 'I'm gonna have to go skunk-crazy,' drag out that *crazy* with hand movements and eye-popping 'tude. I want to see your neck do that wiggle thing. Your expressions will give the artists ideas of how to draw the skunk."

Disbelief had Stacy rooted to the spot. Reynaldo's impression of inner-city life floored her. She already had a bad feeling about the project. When he decided to act it out, she knew that her decision had been correct. This was not for her. She refused to sell her name, voice or reputation to playing a 'hood skunk.

"Reynaldo, I think we need to talk…privately." Stacy put down the script, giving him a heads-up as to the nature of their discussion.

"Looks like we may have a difficult diva," Reynaldo joked with the others.

Stacy waited for him to give her his undivided attention. Something about his demeanor struck a nerve. Holding her temper in check could be an impossible feat.

"What's the problem, Watts?" Reynaldo pinned her with a stare that held no warmth.

"I have a problem with…um…perpetuating stereotypes." Stacy took a deep breath and plunged ahead. "Kids will be watching this. Whether I like this or not, I'm some of these kids' role model. With all the power that you have, don't you feel it your duty to—"

"Don't take it upon yourself to lecture me!" Reynaldo turned a deep tomato-red. "I'm doing a favor to Brenda and frankly, from what I've seen, I can go find another person hungry for this opportunity. You won't last long in this business, so I suggest that you wake up and eat the crumbs that are thrown your way."

Conversation at the table ceased as his voice grew in volume. Stacy's ears burned from a good dose of embarrassment and a mega dollop of rage. She wanted to tell this man where to jump. Her heart beat painfully against her chest as she struggled to control her temper. How long would she have to put up with disrespect and ridicule?

Without addressing Reynaldo's latest comment, she walked over to the table and picked up her pocketbook, being careful to push aside the script. She wanted no reminder from this day, although the experience had made a permanent mark in her memory.

She walked out of the room without addressing anyone. She hadn't made it to the elevator before her cell phone rang. "Yes, Brenda."

"What in the world has gotten into you? You seem to be on a one-way path to killing your career. I thought we had talked through all your angst. But now you've embarrassed me. Do you know what it took for me to get you this audition? Did you ever think about anyone else beyond you? You're successful, but still vulnerable. This business is subjective, and you know this."

Stacy walked into the elevator cab, hoping that the cell phone power would die. It didn't. As she made it down to the lobby, Brenda's fury poured through the tiny device. The doors slid open and

Stacy realized that Brenda had stopped talking. "Hello?"

A wheezing gasp was the only reply.

"Brenda?"

"Call 911." Brenda's voice faded.

Chapter 10

Stacy immediately hung up and called the number for emergencies and then called Brenda's secretary. Then she hopped in a cab and headed for Brenda's office, hoping that she'd beat the ambulance there.

Stacy tried to think of all the things she needed to do, but it was impossible. Brenda had looked fine. But if something was wrong, Brenda wasn't the type to share. Her manager aced at playing the mother, but didn't allow anyone else to switch to that role.

The taxi couldn't move fast enough. The traffic appeared to go against everything she wanted. Stacy debated getting out and running the three remaining blocks down the road, anything to get to Brenda.

As if in answer to her prayer, the traffic started flowing. Traffic lights turned green. She didn't even mind the whopper taxicab fee when the driver finally pulled up to the building. She provided payment with a fat tip and hurried to Brenda.

Stacy headed into the office. Brenda was on the floor. Brenda's secretary knelt at her boss's side, stroking her hand. Tears rolled down her face as she begged Brenda to respond.

"Have the paramedics arrived?" she asked the woman.

She shook her head. "But I've been with her. She's regained consciousness, and she's trying to talk, but nothing is coming out."

"It's okay, I'm here now. Keep an eye out for the paramedics." Stacy waited for the secretary to leave before sinking to her knees beside Brenda. "I'm so sorry," she began. She could feel the emotion building as her throat choked. "You've got to get better to kick my butt." She squeezed Brenda's hand, waiting for an answer. There wasn't any. Brenda's eyes never shifted toward her. Their vacant stare scared Stacy.

The paramedics rushed in, and she stepped aside to give them full access.

"What's wrong with her?" Stacy asked, full of impatience.

"Who found her?" a paramedic asked, as he took her vitals.

"I was on the phone with her, and then she stopped talking." Stacy explained further details about the call.

The paramedic then turned to the secretary who stood in the doorway. "Was she unconscious when you saw her?"

"Yes. I thought she wasn't breathing at first. I don't know how to do CPR. I kept hitting her chest, but I didn't know what to do. Then she took a deep breath and opened her eyes." The secretary sobbed. "I thought that she was okay, but then she wasn't blinking or looking at me."

"Her pulse is low. Her heart is beating irregularly. We're heading to St. Joseph's."

"I'll meet you there." Stacy steered the secretary to the front desk. "I'll need you to go through Brenda's schedule and cancel her appointments. Just say that she had to attend to an urgent matter. Oh, and please cancel my appointments, too." Stacy gave the secretary her information. There was no way that after the tumultuous day and Brenda's condition, she was going anywhere.

Stacy didn't like going to hospitals. Unlike

most people who might have suffered some traumatic experience, she hadn't. Instead the smell of disinfectants mixed with people's illness and scents reminded her of a couple of shelters she'd called home.

"Miss Watts?" A woman in a white doctor's gown approached her.

Stacy didn't like the closed expression.

"I'm Dr. Watkins. Brenda is a relative? Your mother?"

"No. There isn't anyone." The words sounded strange to Stacy's ears.

"Brenda has had a mild heart attack. She has been unresponsive mainly out of shock. I can tell that she's not the type of person who accepts being ill."

Stacy nodded, glad to hear that the news wasn't altogether dire.

"We can perform angioplasty. She's hesitant, though—"

"I'll talk to her," Stacy interrupted.

"You may go see her. By the way, what are you to Brenda?"

"A friend," Stacy said simply, although at this moment, she wished that she could say daughter.

Her heels clicked along the linoleum floor past partially opened doors. Although she was in a section of the ward for very ill patients, there was a flurry of activity and a noise level that defied morose silence.

"She's in a private room. She said that she was leaving if she had to share with anyone," the doctor whispered.

"That sounds like her."

"I hope that she continues to be a fighter because she will need it for the next few months."

Stacy didn't need further explanation. Brenda was lucky to be given a second chance. As guilty as she felt with being the cause of Brenda's collapse, she was grateful that she had been on the phone with her. The alternative was frightening.

The doctor stopped in front of a room. "I'll let you visit. I'll stop by in a bit. Good luck." She shook Stacy's hand and turned away, already focused on another case.

Stacy took a deep breath and walked in. She pasted on what she hoped was a bright smile and greeted Brenda with sickening good cheer.

"Oh, stop it. You're not talking to a baby." Brenda glared at her.

"Well, that depends, doesn't it?" Stacy point-edly looked at the beeping machines, the IV drip-ping into her vein, the oxygen tube under her nose.

"I was simply tired. Needed a break. You and all my high-maintenance clients have worn me out."

Stacy took the only seat in the room. She didn't

know how to convince this stubborn woman to take the extra help. "Do you want me to try and find your daughter?"

"Why do you ask?" Brenda looked shocked.

"Thinking about someone who may sway you to have the surgery."

"Why would someone I haven't seen in years, who pushed me away as a mother, be able to say anything about my life?" Brenda closed her eyes, then reopened them. "You are as close to a daughter as I will ever have."

Stacy was touched. Tears burned at her eyes.

"Oh, stop blubbering over there. I'm not dying."

"Maybe not right now, but if you don't take care of yourself, you could have a more severe heart attack. Your heart is like a ticking time bomb."

"Okay, Miss Mary Sunshine, you can tone it down."

"Brenda, please have the procedure done. It's a simple thing. Technology is so far advanced now, you can't simply brush this aside."

"Since when have you become the doctor? Simple," Brenda huffed. "What do you know?"

"She knows what I told her." The doctor entered the room. Again, no smile was in evidence. Maybe she got her patients to obey her orders because of the no-nonsense attitude that oozed from her.

"Should I call the wrestling federation and sign you up as the new tag-team sensation?"

"Have you made a decision?" the doctor asked.

"You're not opening me up," Brenda said emphatically.

Stacy's phone rang, causing her to hold back a response to Brenda's hardheadedness. She turned into the corner of the room to hide the fact that she was using her cell phone in a hospital. "Hello?" She'd missed looking at the telephone number to identify her caller.

"Hey, babe, where are you?"

Stacy held her other ear to block out the noise. There was so much background noise, listening proved difficult. "Where are *you?*"

"The airport. I thought I'd surprise you. Tried you at home, but since you weren't there, I figured you'd headed to the airport. Have you gone through security?"

"Oh, Omar, gosh, I feel like a heel. There was an emergency. Brenda had a—"

"Don't you tell that boy my business. You're acting as if I'm not in the room." Brenda wheezed between her words.

"Calm down, Brenda." Stacy tried to quiet her. The doctor assisted by talking about the procedure that she wanted to do the next day.

"I'll be staying at the hospital tonight," Stacy told Omar.

"No, you won't, at least not in my room. I don't need you blabbing at me all night, nor do I want to listen to your snoring," Brenda continued to complain.

"I'll leave if you do what needs to be done." Stacy held her hand over the phone's mouthpiece.

"I would call you a name if the doctor wasn't here." Brenda looked at the attending nurse who entered the room to take her vitals.

"I want to hear you say you'll have the angioplasty," Stacy pressed.

"Fine. Do whatever you want." Brenda threw up her hand in surrender.

"Good decision." Stacy resisted the urge to pump a fist in the air.

"Now, you, go away." Brenda pointed at Stacy. "I'm tired."

Stacy turned her attention to her phone. "Sorry about that. Looks like I'm heading home."

"I'll meet you there," Omar replied.

"See, Doc, as soon as he calls, she goes running."

Stacy ignored Brenda's ribbing. Instead she focused on the doctor's plan of action.

Omar couldn't help feeling pleased that Stacy wasn't gone. Brenda might be prickly, but he couldn't get over the fact that such a strong woman had a vulnerable heart. He walked down the hallway to Stacy's door, a little disconcerted that he found himself planning his schedule around her. Was he turning into a whipped boy? His friends would kick him out of the club if they ever got wind of how hard he'd fallen for this woman.

"Hey, I'm heading to the trash room. Make yourself comfortable." Stacy popped a quick kiss on his cheek and rushed past him.

"I can do that," he offered.

"That's okay. I'll remember to save the heavy stuff for you." Stacy continued down the hall, her ponytail dancing with each step.

Omar stepped into Stacy's condo. A spicy scent greeted him, making him think of pumpkin pie or cinnamon toast. The curtains were drawn and the room was lit with muted white light. With her beige and natural furniture colors, the general atmosphere elicited an instant sense of calm. His stressful day slipped further away. He settled on the couch, listening for Stacy's return.

"Hey, sleepyhead." Stacy handed him a cup of coffee. "Just brewed for you."

Omar stretched and miserably failed at stifling a yawn. "Can't believe I dozed. I sat, waited for you, then zoned out while looking at the lighted candle on the coffee table."

"I'm cool. I wasn't giving you a hard time. Are you sticking around for dinner?"

Omar tested the air, frowning.

"I've only started on the noodles." She punched his arm playfully. "I'm making spaghetti."

"Wow, this'll be the first time that you've cooked me a meal." His stomach growled with full appreciation. His taste buds watered at the thought of a hot meal.

"Don't push your luck," she called over her shoulder, as she headed into the kitchen.

Omar listened to the sounds of pots clanging and cabinet doors closing. The quiet whoosh of the refrigerator introduced the sounds of plastic bags rustling. He was too young for domesticity. Yet a part of him liked the thought of long-term commitment. He reached for the remote. There had to be a game on somewhere.

"Nope. No TV tonight. As a matter of fact, you can help mè with the vegetables."

"Vegetables? I thought we were having spaghetti." Omar didn't relish the thought of eating a plateful of veggies.

Stacy had her hand on her hip until he walked into the kitchen. "Now I know you have got to be kidding. Don't you eat mushrooms, green peppers, onions and a little green onions in your spaghetti?"

"Good grief, no. If you buy the high-end brand, it has all of those ingredients in there without me having to see big chunks floating in my spaghetti sauce."

"Get to work. I can see that I'll have to teach you a few things."

"Promise." Omar winked, always ready for a little verbal foreplay.

"Keep your mind on your task. Here's an onion for you to chop."

He might not be the best cook in town, but he knew the effects of chopping onions. He pulled out the largest knife, set the onion on the cutting board, closed his eyes and randomly attacked the vegetable. When he thought it was safe, he opened his eyes. As far as he was concerned, it was a job well done. He slid the board toward Stacy, who had stopped washing the mushrooms to witness his culinary skill.

"Anything else?" he asked, preening from his accomplishment.

"Green peppers next." She tossed him two large peppers.

In under an hour, Omar helped Stacy prepare a pot of thick sauce bubbling on the stove. She tended to the garlic bread warming in the oven. Now familiar with the kitchen, he grabbed plates and silverware to set the table. Instead of placing them at opposite ends of the table, he set their places side by side. He wanted her within reach, to feel her body warmth next to his, to remark on her light, crisp perfume and to play with the soft tendrils of hair near her ears.

No sooner had he set down the glasses than the phone rang. The answering machine picked up the call, playing Stacy's standard greeting and request for a message. She paused in taking out the bread, her head cocked to one side as she listened. Omar found himself also waiting to hear the mysterious caller.

"Stacy, are you there? Stacy, pick up." A voice that clearly belonged to a man insisted on Stacy picking up the phone.

She hadn't moved from her position in front of the stove. Her hands gripped the oven mitt, clutching it close to her chest. The phone rang again, startling her.

Omar walked over to the phone. He'd had enough of this person. He didn't like to think that there was another man interested in Stacy. But more than that, whoever this man was he was clearly upsetting Stacy.

"No. Don't." Stacy pulled back his hand from reaching the phone. "It's Antonio." She wrung the oven mitt like a three-year-old with a rag doll.

"Here, I'll deal with him." Omar took the phone, his temper soaring at this man's tenacity. Through gritted teeth, he barked, "What is your problem?"

"Who's this?" Antonio asked.

"Never mind. Keep up this harassment and you'll end up in court."

"Oh, it's lover boy. Are you going to ride in on your horse to save the poor little rich girl?" Antonio laughed.

Omar realized that this idiotic man was drunk. The fact didn't relax him, knowing that Antonio could brashly do something stupid. "Sleep it off."

"Here, let me talk to him. I can calm him." Stacy reached for the phone.

"I think the bread is burning." Omar motioned toward the oven. When she turned to tend to the stove, he slammed down the phone.

"Darn it. The bread is ruined." Stacy tossed it into the trash. "This meal sucks." She threw up her hands in frustration.

He detected a slight quiver in her voice. "It'll be all right. I won't let him hurt you."

"You don't understand." Stacy sank down into the chair at the table. She lowered her head into her hands.

Omar bit back his frustration. He grew tired of

the mysterious pull that her ex had on her. Did he have to worry about Antonio, the ex-manager, or Antonio, the ex-boyfriend? "Why don't you make me understand?"

Stacy took a deep breath and dragged her hands down her face. "Antonio is that part of my life that I want to set aside. I want people to see and judge me for me. Instead, my background is the topic of conversation in the media."

"You can't change who you are or where you came from. I know, I've tried," he joked weakly. "Find something good about your life to focus on."

"That's priceless." Stacy got up and headed for the refrigerator. "Want a drink?"

"Sure." Omar could use a stiff drink. Much to his surprise, she offered him a glass of milk. He took it, choosing not to be picky.

Stacy resumed her seat, her fingers wrapped tightly around the glass. "I want to work with an organization that focuses on homeless youth."

Omar nodded, sensing that she wasn't finished talking. He sipped his milk and fought the urge to gag. Milk wasn't his favorite beverage.

"When I was on the street, I tried to live with the other street kids, scraping a living working odd jobs for pay under the table." She shook her head, her lips turned down with distaste. "It's not for the fainthearted, let me tell you. Those kids had a higher chance of using drugs. I guess they had to dull the emotional pain that ultimately drove them to leave their homes and families."

Slowly Omar approached her and slid his arm around her shoulders. "Let's sit over here." He didn't know how to comfort her other than to literally offer his shoulder for her to lean her head on. She complied, her body molded to his as they walked. Once they were settled, with Stacy resting her head against his chest, he stroked her hair, tracing the strands from the top of her head to the curled tips. "I'm listening," he said.

"Compared to the other kids, I wasn't homeless for a long time. Guess I knew that I could submit to the foster system if I needed. Otherwise I felt like I was a faceless, nameless character in a macabre play of life."

"And rapping?" Omar coaxed.

"Hip-hop is on the rise, as you know. Every street corner is littered with colorful flyers with talent shows, agents advertising, promoters highlighting key clients. I dragged my feet about writing down the information, then time passed before I actually followed up on the addresses."

"That wasn't very smart," Omar scolded before he could stop himself. "Sorry."

"Hey, now that I look back at that and various other things, I'm lucky to have come out relatively normal. So I headed to auditions and got slammed. Television audiences complain nowadays about that acid-tongued British music producer being cold and heartless. They haven't seen anything. The men, and they were all men, wanted me to rap dressed as if I had an identity crisis. When I started to sing, then they wanted me to dress and act like a Vegas showgirl. That wasn't happening, either. I may have been lacking in social etiquette, but it only took one fight with an all-girl gang to make me realize that only I could care for me."

"That sounds so definite."

"What is there to consider?" She turned to look at him with raised eyebrows.

"Me." Omar met her eyes. He made no attempt to hide that he deeply cared about her. "You've been the tough girl ever since I first met you. I admire that trait, but it's not always necessary."

"Have you ever been let down? Has anyone ever broken your heart?" She barely waited for his response before she continued. "See? Just what I thought, you have no idea how hard it is to let someone take control."

"I'm not asking to take over running your life. You've pretty much done that with Brenda." Omar didn't mean to sound as though he was launching accusations, yet Brenda's objections had seemed narrowly focused on men or more specifically, against him.

"Look, I don't want to fight over this. I appreciate what you're trying to do for me. Although it appears that I can't appreciate it, that's not true." She took his hand and placed it against her upper chest, covering his hand with hers. "You have a special place in my heart."

Omar didn't wait for her to phrase her rejection of his overtures as a confidant. His arms engulfed her and scooped her into a sweeping embrace before his head descended to meet her upturned face. Shock gave way to a subtle moan as Stacy returned his kiss with feverish abandon.

"You make it so difficult for me to make sense whenever you kiss me." Stacy pushed away from him. "What are you doing to me?"

"Loving you." No sooner had the words left Omar's mouth than he buckled under all the weight and pressure of such an admission. "I don't mean love in the sense of Shakespeare." He felt his ankles sink in the quicksand and he struggled to pull himself free. "I like you as a friend. I'm not trying to take advantage of you with empty words about love. I'm certainly not ready to love," he scoffed. Stacy's frown grew deeper. His anxiety escalated. No longer ankle deep, he'd sunk knee deep into this one. "Maybe I should start over."

His brain refused to come to his rescue with a
funny quip to ease the tension.

"It's okay," Stacy reassured him, as she backed
away. She looked over to the table. "Looks like
dinner is over."

"I'm waist deep now."

"Excuse me?" she inquired, her frown returning over his remark.

"Talking to myself. I'll head out now." Omar
hoped that she would tell him to stay. It would soothe
the guilt at bungling his feelings in a manic way.

Omar got his coat and headed for the door.

"I want to work with homeless teens, especially
girls. I want to catch them before they rush into decisions where they use their bodies," Stacy blurted.

"Nothing wrong with that." Omar remained
standing near the door. He honestly didn't see
anything wrong with the idea, but from the hesitation in Stacy's voice, something bothered her.
"Can I help?"

Stacy shook her head. "Sorry, I have to work
out my demons with my own steam." She waved
goodbye. "And I'm not sure that I want you all in
my business." She pushed him through the door.

"Too late." He grinned.

Stacy closed the door. Her dinner with Omar
had fallen apart, along with everything else in her

life. And with regard to Brenda, what a mess she had made of that situation!

Guilt drove her to sit at her desk and write a letter. She poured her heart into each sentence, hoping for a happy outcome. Even after she reread the page, her confidence did a tap dance between disaster and traumatic experience. But she had put off the inevitable for too long.

The only way to complete her self-imposed mission was to call the one man she'd hoped never to call for anything, much less a favor. She dialed star-69 and waited for the computerized voice to provide the telephone number. As she wrote the number on a slip of paper, she agonized over what reopening the door to the past would bring forth.

"I can't believe it," Antonio mocked after she identified herself. "The princess must want something awfully bad for her to chisel the ice from around her heart and call me."

Stacy tried to focus on what she needed from him. Otherwise, she would slam down the phone at his taunting. "I need to find someone."

"Oh, so that's it. You didn't call to tell me that you'd made a mistake with your choice of management."

Stacy squeezed her eyes shut, wishing that he wouldn't rehash their public breakup and his cruel remarks about her worth. "I need to find Valerie."

"Well, isn't that interesting? All this time and now you want to find Valerie. What happened? Your conscience biting a chunk out of your cute behind?"

"Look! Do you know where she is or not?" The one thing about insults was that she had heard them so many times when she worked under Antonio that she had built thick defensive walls.

"Yes, I know where she is. Meet me at Ferentino's and I'll give you the information."

"I'm not making any deals with you," Stacy replied crossly.

"Eight o'clock tonight."

His timing meant that she had less than an hour before meeting him. "I want us to meet in the daytime at a place of my choosing."

"And I want to be your man, instead of that young boy you string along."

"That's not happening."

"And neither is your wish. Be there at eight."

The phone line disconnected. A whirlwind of emotions rolled around and bounced off each other. Each reverberation had an effect as if a thousand bees hovered over her head aimed to do damage beyond what she could handle.

Against her better judgment, she grabbed her car keys and left her apartment. Her pulse hurried along with her uneven pace, while she prayed for a happy ending, but dreaded what she might have to endure.

Chapter 11

Omar sat in his car, staring up at Stacy's condo. He knew that he should go to her and hammer out whatever their problems were. His hesitation crippled him and any attempt at a relationship. He had turned off the engine and opened the car door when he saw Stacy's light go out.

He paused, a bit surprised that she could go off to bed with no apparent deliberation. Maybe he should follow suit and head home and stop acting like a lovesick teen. He restarted the engine, and waited for traffic to go past.

The condo-building door swooshed open and

Stacy stepped out, pulling her jacket closed against the night breeze. "Where the heck is she going?" Omar questioned aloud. He looked at the time displayed on the radio panel. It wasn't technically late, but if they had continued on with their dinner plans that night, she wouldn't have been stepping out, unless an emergency had cropped up about Brenda.

Either way, he waited until she got into her car and pulled off. He felt like a stalker driving several car lengths behind her. When she turned onto Peachtree Street away from the hospital, he stopped feeling guilty.

Now he was just plain curious. He kept a hold on the jealous twinges poking at his ego. No need to jump to conclusions unnecessarily. However, he definitely wasn't going home now. Following Stacy's actions, he parked his car and headed for the Italian restaurant she had entered.

Omar had seen enough movies of one person spying on the betrayal by another in a restaurant setting. Although they had not officially declared themselves as boyfriend-girlfriend, he and Stacy certainly had enjoyed each other's company exclusively. Even in his more active dating period, he'd ended his relationships before embarking on the next journey, no matter how short.

Standing on the sidewalk looking in on the

busy, hectic scene of diners and waiters, he was reduced to spying on Stacy. He followed her path, escorted by a chatty waitress, as they weaved among the scattered tables and diners to the far end of the expansive room. Omar craned his neck to see whom she greeted, but the person remained in the shadows. For a few seconds, he contemplated going into the restaurant, then he walked into the well-lit lobby.

"Good evening, sir. How many?" the host asked.

"One." Omar self-consciously straightened his shirt.

"It will be about a ten-minute wait, sir."

Omar shook his head, totally frustrated with this development.

"How about the bar? If you don't mind sitting there for your meal."

Omar looked in the direction of the bar, gauging its distance to where Stacy was. He still couldn't see her dinner partner clearly, although he would give a good guess that it was a man. "I'll pass on the bar, thanks." He turned to leave.

"Sorry about that, sir," the host said, providing his obligatory statement of regret.

Omar nodded and exited the building. He turned down the sidewalk that would take him past Stacy's table. At this point he didn't care if she saw him.

"Sir! Sir! We have a table." The host stood in the doorway waving at him.

"Where is the table situated?" Omar asked irritably.

"Sir?"

Omar was past caring whether he appeared rude. He could walk around the sidewalk and satisfy his curiosity or end up sitting at the back of the restaurant with a hefty bill for his trouble.

The host waited in the doorway, clearly not committing to an answer.

"That's okay. Maybe another night." Omar turned and continued on his way toward the end of the block. In an effort to appear to be an ardent admirer of architecture, he strolled down the sidewalk surveying the large windows.

One windowpane framed Stacy perfectly. One step to the left and he saw her dinner partner. "Antonio?"

"Excuse me?" A passerby stopped with a questioning frown.

"Sorry, talking to myself." Omar gave a half-hearted chuckle.

The passerby offered a knowing smile, but nevertheless, crossed at the next intersection.

He returned his attention to the window. The conversation had became so animated that they were drawing the attention of other diners. Omar recognized Stacy's tight body language. She radiated anger. Antonio had a plate filled with food, while Stacy merely had a glass of water. Her hands performed a lively dance to match the strong, animated expressions appearing and vanishing on her face.

Reading lips had never been part of his repertoire. Stacy carried most of the conversation, with Antonio leaning back casually. The usual annoying smirk sat upon his face. Occasionally he filled his fork and delicately ate.

Quite suddenly, Stacy threw down her napkin and shot up, forcefully pushing back her chair. Antonio made no move to stop her. Instead he stared at her while chewing.

In a matter of seconds, Stacy burst out of the restaurant. Omar didn't hide, but also didn't step forward. She was clearly upset as she hurried to her car. Her keys already in hand, she opened the door and slid in quickly. Omar returned his gaze to Antonio, who was having his wineglass refilled.

Without deliberating any further, Omar found himself standing in front of Antonio. He rested his hand on the chair Stacy had occupied only moments ago. "Antonio, may I join you?" Before Antonio recovered from his shock, Omar pulled out the chair and sat.

"I suspect that this is not a coincidence."

Antonio signaled to a waiter. "Since you're already seated, would you like a glass of wine? Maybe it will relax that murderous scowl that you have for me."

Omar slid Stacy's water aside for the waiter to remove. He ordered a glass of Chardonnay.

"Try the veal parmesan. Freaking fantastic." Antonio cleared his plate, then pushed it aside.

"I'll pass." Omar leaned forward and rested his elbows on the table. "Let's get right down to why I'm here."

"Your insecurity, perhaps?"

Omar didn't react, although he would have enjoyed nothing better than to reach over the votive candle to Antonio's tie and surrender to a primal urge to kick his butt.

"You're worried about nothing. Sit a spell. I'll fill you in." Antonio grinned, openly showing his enjoyment of the current situation.

Stacy drove toward home, away from the hectic bustle of the nightclubs and high-end restaurants. She had picked her residence with the intention that her previous lifestyle would always be at her back. Her balcony looked toward the suburbs of Atlanta.

Now her past incessantly knocked for entry into her present circumstances. Brenda thought that she should profit from her past. Omar thought that she should embrace who she was. Antonio wanted to taunt her with the life she had left behind.

The taunting worked to unnerve her. The information he tossed her way like loose change battered her conscience. She dropped her keys on the kitchen counter and headed to her room. She couldn't wait to get out of her clothes and jump into the shower and scrub away Antonio's leering propositions. The man couldn't take no for an answer, but he knew too much about her secrets and could be a destructive force in her life.

As she dried off, her phone rang, a unique buzz, alerting her that it was the concierge's desk in the lobby. She looked at the clock. If Antonio had followed her, she would not hesitate to call the police. Now that she had the information she sought, she had a plan forming in her mind to neutralize any threat from him.

"Miss Watts, you have a visitor—Omar Masterson."

"He came back?" Stacy frowned.

"Pardon?"

"Send him up, please." Stacy threw off her robe quickly and pulled on a baggy T-shirt and sweatpants. She managed to restore order to her hair before her doorbell rang.

"Omar, didn't expect to see you so late."

He strode in and scooped her up without a word.

"Whoa," Stacy protested halfheartedly.

"We'll talk afterward."

"After?" Stacy asked, very much aware that they were heading for her bed.

"I don't know what tomorrow may bring us. I don't think you know, either. But right here, right now, we've got something special that I know in my heart is worth whatever we can bring to it."

Stacy looked up at him. His piercing gaze warmed her all over.

"Do you want me? Do you want me now?" Omar pushed.

Stacy nodded. She didn't want to say anything to delay Omar's mouth touching hers.

He laid her down on the bed gently. Her body sank among the pillows and for an instant she imagined that she was in a field of wildflowers with her lover.

"I thought you were mad at me when you left," Stacy managed to say as Omar kissed her neck. She couldn't help the small giggle that escaped when he touched a sensitive spot behind her ear.

"Shh. No more talking." He covered her mouth and gathered her into a deep embrace until she melted against his chest.

"Okay, I won't say a word," she squeaked. Her

body arched to his, making its own language in response to his sensual actions.

"You insist on rebelling against my wishes, woman." Omar planted a series of wet kisses along her neck, down her chest.

"That's because I like the punishment." Stacy held fast to his ears as he nuzzled her breasts. The sensitivity of those peaks caused her to moan as strong sexual urgings coursed through from her nipples down to the moist folds between her thighs.

Stacy enjoyed Omar's attentions, responding and leading her own campaign to dominate his thoughts with her ministrations. His muscles rippled under her touch as she traced his form. Her hand seemed so small against his expansive chest where she circled his nipple with her tongue. Her hands didn't stop their mission as she enjoyed the shape of the thick muscles along his stomach.

Her mind screamed for him to stop teasing her with his wicked tongue. She opened her legs, an invitation that spoke loud and clear. Though she loved the heat of his mouth leaving a blazing trail along her body, she wanted him to attend to the craving between her legs. She wrapped her legs around his hips and arched toward him, beginning their improvised choreography.

Omar surrendered to her yearnings, entering

her with slow, purposeful strokes until he completely filled her. Their bodies communicated in their special, nonverbal language that involved skin touching skin, actions and reactions and throwing out reason and logic. As his powerful thrusts triggered and stroked awake her essence deep at the climactic point, Stacy pushed back any lingering annoyances of reality.

She didn't care what time it was. She didn't want to know what they would do when this was over. Nothing in this evening that led up to Omar's visit had any place in her consciousness.

Instead she listened to the rising level of her desire in response to Omar's quickened strokes. She hung on to him, tightening her hips against his as they rode each orgasmic wave together with a fierce, frenetic speed. Her body twitched from each explosion, further scrambling her thoughts. All she could manage was to emit a happy moan as she rode the crest to the end.

Stacy hurried out of the studio building, looking forward to her dinner with Omar. All day she had floated from the aftereffects of a wonderful evening in his arms. She couldn't resist humming throughout the day and even managed a quick step or two as she grabbed her coat after her final meeting with the studio execs.

A horn blew several times as she craned to see if Omar was waiting as they had planned. He'd said that he wanted to talk, which was perfectly fine with her if it ended in the same manner as last night. Just as she was about to pull out her cell phone, she saw the familiar car.

"Hey." She greeted Omar with a quick kiss on the side of his mouth.

"Hungry?" Omar asked, as he drove through the afternoon traffic.

Stacy nodded. "I'm in the mood for Thai."

"I know this great place that may look like a hole, but the food is fantastic." Omar steered the car through the crowded street, until the ramp for the highway appeared.

"How was your day?" Stacy asked. "I think that I was too perky for some people today." She leaned her head against the headrest with a satisfied smile.

Omar gave her hand a small squeeze. "I actually played hookey today. Needed a mental-health day."

"What? And you didn't call me?"

"Don't worry, I didn't do anything fun."

"Yeah, right. It was a gorgeous day. Even the weather was warmer than I thought it would be." Stacy pulled at her coat with disgust.

"Okay, now you're making me feel guilty."

Omar called the restaurant to find out the wait time and leave their name for a reservation. "It's a forty-five-minute wait, but I'm game if you are."

"Is it the sort of place where we can sit around?"

"Actually there's a park nearby. We can probably get a good few minutes' walk before dusk."

"Then let's go," Stacy said.

At the park, there were several families bundling up their children, despite their shrill protests. As the young families departed, the young professionals descended in their running gear. Stacy had never fancied herself a jogger. Her form of exercise was in a Jazzercise class in an air-conditioned building.

"Let's grab this bench over here." Omar pointed to an elaborately carved bench facing a fountain whose water had been shut off for the season.

Omar sat first and placed his arm on the back of the bench. Stacy welcomed the chance to sit close to his body, inhaling his cologne.

"We can't throw a penny into the fountain to make a wish," Stacy complained.

"Is there a rule that there must be flowing water?" Omar reached into his pocket and pulled out two coins. "Here, you take one."

"Nope. It must be my coin or you might get my wish."

Omar tilted up her chin and dropped a knee-buckling kiss on her lips. Only the chatter of passing joggers stopped her from holding on and returning his kiss with one of her own. She could certainly give as good as she got.

Omar tossed a coin, which bounced off the metalwork of the fountain and landed on the tiled bottom.

Stacy observed him close his eyes. His lips moved silently. She waited for his eyes to open. "I know that you can't tell me what you wished for, but what's the category?"

"Your turn," he responded, ignoring her question.

Stacy closed her eyes, made her wish, blew into her clasped hand, opened her eyes and tossed in the coin. Omar looked at her with matching anticipation. But she could never tell him what she wished. Partly, she didn't expect the wish to come true, anyway. Also, she couldn't tell him that what she wanted more than anything was to trust him, trust in him. What she had suffered in the past had scarred her and branded her heart and mind in such a way that she didn't know how to release the baggage. Looking up at Omar, feeling the strong emotion in her heart that could only be love, she didn't know how long they would last. One day he just might disappoint her or she might disappoint him.

"Hey, don't go silent on me. I feel as if you're zoning on me." Omar gently nudged her.

Stacy offered him a dreamy smile, pushing back the urge to cry. All of a sudden, she had become a girly-girl with over-the-top emotions and whimsical fantasies. Life wasn't about fairy-tale plots and it was certainly not about happy endings.

"You often wear that sad expression. I wish you would see me as more than a lover."

"But I do." Stacy sat back, more than a little surprised by Omar's criticism. "You are a friend. My friend." She picked up his hand and kissed the top.

"Ah, but you say that, and yet I have difficulty believing that I'm really your friend, a friend in whom you can or share your secrets," he said softly.

"That would be a girlfriend's job."

"And you don't have that, either."

Stacy pushed away from him. "Go ahead. Ask your pesky question."

Omar turned to her and folded his arms. Pinning her with his intense gaze, he asked, "Would you help me on a project?"

"Sure." Stacy relaxed, not expecting him to give up so easily. "It certainly looks like I might have some free time for the next few months since I have missed auditions and turned down a few offers." She shrugged. "Guess I'm taking advantage of Brenda's recuperation." She chuckled, knowing that once her manager felt better, there would be serious consequences.

"I want to have a TV special on the homeless state of young adults. This is the idea that the bigwigs thought was beyond my capabilities."

Stacy's hands stilled their playful games with Omar. Her heartbeat escalated, pumping so hard that she could feel the vibration in her ears. "What do you want me to do?"

"I'd like to have you involved in this."

"Me?" Her voice croaked. "What could I do?"

"Here, let's get to the car before we miss our reservation." Omar stood and held out his hand.

Stacy took his hand. She hated to admit to him that her appetite had fled. Only minutes ago, they'd been teasing and flirting with each other. Now her body stiffened with tension.

"I know and the public knows about your background and how you made the right decisions to move on with your life. And what a success! I think that you could anchor the piece with your personal experiences."

Stacy looked down at her feet, feeling as if she were having an out-of-body experience. "Why is this so important to you?"

"Because I know it's important to you. And I

know how it feels to be seeking your place in this world. I know how easy it is to give up and walk away. And I know how hard it is to work through the tough crap and believe in what is not there."

"I think you see too much good in every thing and every person." Stacy heard what he said, but it didn't make her feel any better. Helping others was one thing, but talking about it on a TV camera was another.

They made it through dinner. Conversation was sparse compared to their lighter, flirtatious moments in the park. Stacy grappled with her decision, as she steered the conversation to safer topics, like Brenda's operation, recovery and pending discharge from the hospital the next day.

"Don't be mad," she pleaded with Omar after they left the restaurant.

"I'm not mad."

Stacy looked at his unsmiling profile as he drove. If he wasn't angry, then she certainly didn't think he was happy. "I truly will think about it."

"I know. Since it makes you uncomfortable, there is no need to justify your decision. I will respect your wishes."

"But I haven't made up my mind," Stacy protested. All she had to say was go ahead and Omar would run with it. Yet taking that courageous step was beyond her capabilities at the moment. "Are we going back to your place?" She hoped that the remainder of the evening would not be forfeited.

"Didn't you have to pick up Brenda early in the morning tomorrow?"

She nodded. She'd forgotten that she'd promised Brenda to be available. At least her housekeeper would do the necessary shopping.

"I have an early meeting and I won't be able to get you home in the morning."

Stacy bit down on her disappointment. He couldn't possibly be holding a grudge.

"Don't read anything into what I just said. I can sense the squeaky, grinding machinery called your brain examining my words."

Stacy laughed, a bit embarrassed at being revealed.

When they pulled up to her condo, Stacy turned to Omar. He really wasn't going to come out of the car. Disappointment seeped in, depressing her thoughts. A frightening thought entered her mind. Was this the issue that could separate them?

Stacy touched Omar's face, trying with all her might, in her nonverbal way, to communicate the extent of her love. She kissed him softly and her heart filled with joy to feel his active response. "Good night," she whispered.

She got out of the car and walked into her building without turning around. Maybe she should be grateful that they were spending the evening in separate homes. She'd never committed her heart to anyone, and the journey was proving to be more difficult than she'd expected.

A few minutes later, a knock on her door caused her to frown. "Yes," she answered, hesitating. "Who is it?" she asked with more force.

"Omar."

She immediately opened the door. Her mood lightened considerably to see him standing before her. "Did I leave something in the car?"

"No." Instead he held his cell phone out toward her. "My brother, Pierce, wants to chat with you."

"Your brother?" Stacy managed to say. Her legs felt weak.

"Don't look so scared." Omar chuckled. "He wants to personally extend an invitation."

Stacy heard Omar, but still didn't understand. She took the phone and turned her back on Omar to hide her discomfort, as she gnawed on her lip. This was his older brother. The last thing she wanted was to sound like a teenager. She cleared her throat.

"Hello, this is Stacy."

"Stacy, how are you? This is Pierce. Omar has talked a lot about you. I think that you've been good for my little brother. You've obviously helped him think about his future. I would love to have you come and meet the rest of the family."

"Oh." Stacy looked at Omar, who was trying to seem interested in her wall art. He was no help. Meeting the family was a big deal. Meeting the family over a weekend could prove to be traumatic.

"Don't worry. We are a harmless bunch. Here, talk to Haley, my wife." Stacy heard the noisy exchange of the phone. She felt as if she were in the middle of a tag team. But there was no one on her end to pass the phone off to. Looking at Omar leaning against her bookcase, trailing a finger over her hardcover collection, she categorized him as a double agent.

"Hi, Stacy, Haley here. Let me apologize for Pierce's heavy-handed invitation."

"Oh, it's okay," Stacy lied. She immediately relaxed at the soothing quality of Haley's voice.

"A family celebrating a birthday could be overwhelming, but it is when we are all together. Laura and her husband will be joining us, which is a big deal since her husband is often competing. I promise not to let them overwhelm you. I was once in your shoes."

Haley laughed and Stacy could only join in with the simple show of empathy. "Thanks for the double invitation. Yes, I won't lie. I am a bit intimidated by all of it. However, I would love to come and meet your family."

"Wonderful. I'll let everyone know. Well, I won't keep you. Give my brother-in-law a kiss. I'll chat with you later."

Stacy ended the call, took a deep breath and handed the phone back to Omar. "Looks like I'll be meeting the Mastersons."

"Thanks for agreeing to come." Omar looked down at his hands. Stacy felt that he had more that he wanted to say. He hesitated, then opened the front door. "I know they will like you and I hope you will like them."

"I'm sure I will."

He kissed her softly on her cheek and left.

Stacy leaned her head against the door. Meeting the entire family scared her. The possibilities of what could go wrong seemed limitless. Her mind played with several excuses that could give her an out, but still let her save face.

Then she'd be starting with a lie. She secretly felt honored to be invited by Omar's big brother. More than ever, she wanted them to be impressed by her. Could they accept her? Not the celebrity image, but the girl from the streets with the blood of her dysfunctional parents running through her veins?

Chapter 12

"Brenda, the doctor hasn't released you to go back to work." Stacy rushed over to Brenda's chair to assist her as she got shakily to her feet. "Even if you're working from home, you're still working."

"Girl, when did you become such a fusspot?" Brenda clucked her tongue, irritation plain on her face. "You're not my only client, although you act as if you are."

Stacy didn't bother to respond. She might not be Brenda's only client, but she was the only one who would take care of her.

"You know, you should get your hairdresser over here," Stacy suggested, fingering Brenda's hair.

"Think I need a touch-up on the color of my roots?" Brenda ran her hands over her short hair.

"At the very least," Stacy remarked drily.

"Fine." Brenda noted the fact on a writing pad. "I've got tons of stuff to work on." She set the pen down with a decisive snap. "Now, young lady, we have to get you busy again. I'm so sorry that things got slow for you."

Stacy shrugged. Granted, she was still earning an income, but she didn't miss going on those awful auditions and facing rejection. "I've been writing a few songs—"

"Why? We have three songwriters working with you. You've never written songs."

"But for this album, I'd like songs that speak to all the feelings trapped inside me. And no one can say it better than me."

"Sometimes you frustrate me."

"And sometimes you smother me."

"Ever since that man walked into your life, you have not been able to concentrate. You act like the first woman to fall in love."

"That's not fair." Stacy desperately tried to restrain her anger. After all, she didn't want Brenda to suffer again.

"You're letting your career flitter away."

"They're still playing my songs. Still showing the music videos. The movie is slated to come out next winter. We're not in a race." Stacy's chest heaved as if she had run a marathon.

Brenda's housekeeper appeared quietly in the room. With minimal fuss, she set down a glass of water and Brenda's midday pills.

"I'm tired of fighting with you. Next month, we have to start talking about the marketing plans for your upcoming album."

"I want to sit in on the talks from beginning to end."

"Of course. I've never prevented you," Brenda said crossly.

Stacy had to agree. Maybe she hadn't taken the initiative, easily feeling overwhelmed. No more.

"But I don't know what theme I want yet," Stacy said.

"Then I guess you'd better get to work. Otherwise, the marketing department will be only too happy to create one for you." Brenda chuckled. "Remember when they wanted you to do the Christmas collaboration album?"

"Don't remind me. I was supposed to wear a Christmas Santa suit that looked like a hoochie-mama outfit and strut down Martin Luther King Jr. Boulevard." Stacy rolled her eyes. "I don't think so."

"Use that thought when you need incentive to work." Brenda looked up at the clock on the mantel. "I need to make a few calls."

"Sure. I've got to head out, anyway. I need to go shopping for gifts." Stacy bit her lip. She had not meant to hint about her upcoming trip to the Mastersons'.

"Someone's birthday?" Brenda looked up at her.

"Um…not really. I'm meeting Omar's family."

"Really! They've come to Atlanta?"

"No. His brother invited me. To their house. In Maryland." Stacy forced herself to be quiet. Or maybe it was the angry vein protruding along Brenda's throat. "Before you begin insulting my intelligence again, I am going."

Brenda opened her mouth, but then shook her head, closed her mouth and turned away.

Stacy read the signs of dismissal and took the cue. Lately she and Brenda could not agree on too many things. Omar was a topic that definitely couldn't withstand a coherent conversation.

"I'll call you later this evening," Stacy said.

"No need. I'll probably be resting."

Stacy lowered her head and left Brenda's house. Once she exited, her spirit felt lighter. She was afraid to think that she no longer wanted to be around Brenda. For some unknown reason,

Brenda seemed bitter and dissatisfied, especially with her.

As she drove away, she looked at the huge, palatial home. Despite its shiny white siding and forest-green shutters, manicured evergreens and lawn and cobblestoned driveway, the residence lacked life, a family.

She personally could identify with that void.

Omar studied his notes after the Monday-morning status reports had been completed. He needed to seclude himself so that he could concentrate on what still needed to be done on his project. He had passed the excitement stage when he'd finally received approval from the powers-that-be to go ahead with his idea.

"You didn't come to get me." Rosa stepped into the room, hesitating only briefly before approaching him at the other end of the table. She looked over his shoulder.

"I would have called you. Decided to grab a few minutes of quiet to go over this last piece."

"The finale? You need to leave with a message."

"I know that," Omar answered impatiently. "I just don't think that it should end with you." Henderson had grudgingly given him the green light to start his project. Their biggest disagreement was Rosa. Omar figured he'd fight the battle later.

"I see." Rosa's voice took on an edge. "I suppose you think you should be the one."

Omar returned his gaze to the papers laid out in order of the sections. Though Rosa irritated him, he also recognized that she could bring a lot of attention to the documentary picture. But this project had to end with someone who had lived the experiences highlighted in the ninety-minute piece.

"I'm going to leave the draft of your script for you. Review it and if there is no problem, then start learning it. I don't have the luxury to cater to numerous outtakes."

Rosa took the papers and nodded. "When can I expect the endnotes?"

"This is it for now." Omar needed her as the interviewer. He didn't need her input to mar his inspiration. Time wasn't on his side, but with quiet to think, he would have it all figured out. His reputation depended on it.

Rosa looked down at the notes and then up at him. "Why do we have to be at the location so early in the morning?"

"We need to be able to get in and out of the downtown area before rush hour begins," he explained. He glanced through the glass walls at the clock over the staff assistants' cubicle. "Darn it. I have to scout another location, then check to see if one of our sources came through for an interview."

"You don't have to do it all. I know you see me as a minor participant on this team. But that's your perception, not the reality." Rosa walked out of the conference room.

Omar watched her walk past with her chin pointing outward. Her displeasure practically oozed off her stiff walk. Frustrated, Omar tossed down his pen and tried to rub the fatigue off his face. He reacted with a tired yawn that had him stretching his long limbs.

This was no time to indulge in his exhaustion. He headed out, willing his mind to focus on the tasks ahead. For the remainder of the morning, he chatted with his producer, then drove to the location, before deciding to call Stacy for a possible lunch date.

Unfortunately, her voice mail came on immediately. He left a message, hoping that she would check in soon. In the meantime, he would work on his main source. Using the computer-generated directions, he drove into Cypress Hills. The area wasn't the best, but he had seen worse.

He parked his car on a side road and offered a quick prayer that it would be intact when he returned. After one last look at his car, he headed for the apartment building.

Kids milled around the front of the renovated-warehouse apartment homes. The girls sat on the wide concrete railings. The boys strutted at the bottom of the stairs on the sidewalk. Their bad-boy images weren't too far from their lives. Omar didn't know if they would allow him to pass without verbal harassment. He wasn't physically intimidated by them, but that didn't mean that he shouldn't be aware.

"Hey, cutie," prompted one of the young girls.

"Good afternoon." Omar deepened his voice to ward off any further quips.

"You don't have to rush off." Another girl took up the baton to harass him.

Omar provided a tight smile, but didn't respond. Maybe that had been his first mistake that drew their attention.

"Hey, man, didn't you hear my girl talking to you?" a young man's voice scolded.

Omar did his best to bulk up, tightening his chest and straightening his shoulders. He erased any trace of a smile and tightened his face with a scowl. "Maybe if she was really your girl, she wouldn't be sitting up here while you're down there."

His peers screamed their approval of Omar's put-down. The young man wasn't amused, especially when the girl stood and taunted him that he'd better not come up before her brother kicked his butt.

Omar used the diversion to head into the apartment. Now that he'd riled the young man, he would probably have to look both ways after he exited. His car, however, was unprotected.

The hallway was dimly lit as a result of several light fixtures without working bulbs. A pungent, clinging odor that turned his stomach hung in the air. Smells of foods native to a multitude of cultures seeped out from under each door and collided in the common area of the building. As Omar climbed the stairs, the smell stayed with him, filling his lungs. He couldn't wait to exit the building and take a deep breath.

After two flights of stairs, he walked down the hall looking for the number that Antonio had given him. If what Antonio had told him was true, several pieces to the puzzle surrounding Stacy would fall into place. He promised himself that no matter what he discovered she would always claim his heart.

"I thought you weren't coming. I was about to change my mind." A young woman stood in her doorway with one hand on her hip. Instead of being glad for the attention, she didn't hesitate to show her irritation with this interruption in her life.

"Valerie?"

"Who else would it be?" She motioned into the

apartment. "Come on in before my nosy neighbors think that I'm sociable."

"Don't want to screw with their minds," he muttered, full of sarcasm.

From her mere appearance, Valerie couldn't possibly be the person he needed to talk to. He'd expected a woman who looked as if she had been slapped around by life's disasters. Instead, Valerie was dressed in a slinky number that glued itself to her skin as if she was about to hit a nightclub. Only problem was that it wasn't even three o'clock. The getup made her look cheap.

Omar stepped over the threshold, suspecting that he would never forget this moment. Valerie closed the door behind him, applying the three locks on the door. Her security measures only served to make him feel like a prisoner.

"Don't have much of anything in here. Move those clothes to the floor and you take the seat."

"That's okay. He leaned against a countertop that divided the kitchen from the dining area. Instead of a dining area, Valerie used the space for a bedroom of sorts. There was a daybed along one wall, a stack of Sunday newspapers and clothing heaped in a corner.

"Don't get much visitors, so didn't bother to clean up." Valerie pointed over the room with no hint of an apology to be seen.

"I'm fine. I won't keep you. As I mentioned on the phone, Antonio gave me your information." Omar cleared his throat. He was surprised to see that she looked well groomed and satisfied, despite the odd clothing choice, considering that she lived on the streets. But within the hour, he hoped to learn more about her.

She pulled over a chair from a two-seater card table and sat. Since she didn't invite him to do the same, he took the initiative and made himself comfortable.

"What burning questions do you want to ask me?" Valerie folded her arms and leaned back with enough attitude.

Omar saw the street edge that she wore as a second skin. Her defenses were raised. If he didn't win her over fast, she would end this conversation right now. "Why did Antonio tell me to ask you about Stacy?"

Her eyes narrowed, suspiciously studying him. "Don't believe that dog." She unfolded her arms and slid her hands along her thighs, flexing and unflexing her fingers. "He tried to get with me after Stacy left him." She paused. "What's it to you?"

"Like I said, I'm working on a documentary for young kids about homeless teens and young adults. I want to use Stacy Watts's story as inspiration for these kids. Antonio said you could shed some light on her beginnings."

Valerie stood and walked around the small apartment with her head lowered to her chest. Every other step, she chuckled.

Omar didn't say anything since he wasn't privy to her source of amusement. "I would like to capture your thoughts on tape." He crossed his fingers that she wouldn't freak out about that since he hadn't given her any forewarning. If she agreed, he had his two-man crew in a van in the area, awaiting his call.

Valerie stopped pacing and returned to her chair. She was no longer chuckling. Instead, she looked sad or maybe bitter. Omar sensed a moment of great revelation about to be made.

"Go ahead, tape me."

Omar wanted to hoot at his success. But he only took out his phone and dialed the number, summoning his team. His pulse revved with subdued excitement as his vision unfolded to reality.

Half an hour later, Omar had the place staged for the interview. Valerie had cleared an area, aided by his prompting, and now sat against the wall with a poster of Stacy on it. They'd had to scramble to find tape to create the backdrop.

"Please tell me your name and relationship to Stacy."

"Valerie Marie Buxton. Guess you can call me a childhood friend."

"You don't count yourself as her friend any longer?"

Valerie shrugged. "It's not like we had a fight or something. I mean, she went her way." She looked around the room. "Guess I stayed."

"How did you come to meet her?"

"We met at a homeless shelter in Miami. You get to know the people around you. We'd hang out, dodge the cops, stay away from those social worker types."

"So you became instant friends?"

"You could say that."

"How long did you live on the streets?" Omar gestured to their space. "You do have a roof over your head now?"

"I lived on the streets for about three years. Sometimes I did end up back at home, but not for long."

"Life was tough at home?"

Valerie sneered. "Tough isn't half of it. I was supposed to be perfect. You know the motto, like mother, like daughter. Too much pressure. Plus I wasn't interested in all that crap. When my parents separated, I wanted to go live with my father. He said that a girl should be raised by her mother. If I was a boy, he would have taken me."

Omar sensed that he had moved from her air of indifference to a very sensitive part of her life. His ability to navigate through the murky tangle of hurt and anger was important. He couldn't rely on his experience as a journalist or an interviewer to get through this. Just as she had turned inward to share her pain, he would also have to pull on his emotions to empathize with her.

"Abandonment is never easy," he consoled. "Maybe your mother felt that she had to be tough as a way to hide her hurt and to protect you from what she knows is out there."

Valerie's expression hardened. "The great Brenda Young has no heart. She worried more about what others would think about me, her wild daughter, than what I was going through." Valerie's voice rose in anger. Her gaze drifted off to the side as if she was reliving some tumultuous episode.

"Brenda Young is your mother!" Omar hadn't moved beyond that startling fact. His mouth was open in disbelief. He turned to his team to share this stunning news, but then realized that the news meant nothing to them. "Then how did Stacy get with your mother…" Omar frowned as if the puzzle seemed so close to a solution, but a few pieces had shifted.

"Stacy was getting hot on the street-music

scene. She had the look, the voice and Antonio, who served his purpose to get her into lots of underground clubs and competitions. Then my mother popped up on the scene trying to find me."

"Brenda came looking for you?"

"She'd hired a detective and then when he found me, he told her. But word traveled fast and I knew she was in the area before she could get out of her fancy car. I'll give it to her, she stuck around for a bit. Sometimes, she moved on to the next area, but then she'd come right back."

"Maybe it's one of the mother-daughter bonds where she could sense that you were nearby."

Valerie snorted. "You're such a softie. It wasn't about me. It was about Stacy. She sniffed the wind and smelled success."

"You feel that she picked Stacy over you?"

"Nah. Like I said, she didn't know I was in the area. But one thing I do know is that my mother can turn things into gold. So I told Stacy how to get her attention. Then the rest was no big deal. When my mother made the offer to take her on, the only obstacle was Antonio. But as I predicted, my mother rolled out the cash and took care of business."

"But Antonio is calling foul," Omar interjected.

"I bet he is. All his acts have left him because he's not about taking someone to the next level. Stacy was loyal, but he would have used her up."

"Sounds like you don't resent her for leaving you."

Valerie didn't say anything. She bit her lip, not quite meeting his eyes. He saw the telltale tremble of her bottom lip. He had no clue what to do if she started crying.

"Um…do you want to take a quick break?" Omar asked.

Valerie shook her head. She looked down at her watch. "We don't have much time. Let's get through this."

"Okay. Did Stacy ever tell your mother?"

"Don't know." Valerie paused. "If she did, my mother never came to find me."

"But you know where to find either of them."

"I don't fit in their world now. When Stacy was here, she was my homegirl. Now she's a star. She's the one my mother is proud of. I've got my life here. I don't need either one of them, you know what I mean?"

Omar shook his head. "I think you're undervaluing your relationship with your mother. She is the one who came after you." He didn't have to say that her father wasn't the one walking up and down the sidewalks looking for his daughter.

His father had left home. He had simply gotten in his car and left. Not even his mother's funeral had brought back his father.

"Did Stacy ever come to see you?" Omar asked, his own emotion choking him.

"In the beginning, she'd visit. I'd get to stay in a clean hotel for a couple days. She'd worry about me, though. I had to promise that I wouldn't start taking drugs."

"Did you keep that promise?"

"Yes, I'm no drug user," she replied crossly.

"Would you want to see Stacy?" Omar didn't know why he put the invitation out there when he didn't have a clue how he could make it happen.

Valerie looked around her apartment. "Yeah, I guess. I'm off the streets. I have a home. Nothing like what she probably has, though."

"A home is more than the walls and roof," Omar reassured her.

At that moment, a noise at the door interrupted the interview. They turned to the sound of a key being inserted into a lock. Omar looked from the door to Valerie, wondering why she wasn't doing something about this home invasion. For all he knew, the same young guy he'd humiliated could be on the other side with his friends ready to take him down. He stood, prepared to defend the space.

The door opened. Omar stiffened.

A man with a sleeping infant on his shoulder came through the door. Omar and the man exchanged looks of surprise before turning to Valerie for an explanation.

"Baby, this is Omar Masterson," she explained.

Omar offered his hand, knowing how strange it must all look with him and the microphone and his team with the camera and light on her, with no apparent reason for the attention.

The man shook his hand. "Vince."

Omar waited for the last name, but after the lengthy pause, knew that it wasn't forthcoming. With the scrutiny fluctuating between suspicion and hostility, he knew better than to suggest that Vince participate in the interview.

Valerie walked up to Vince and took the sleeping bundle. "This is my pride and joy."

"You have a baby."

"Our baby," Valerie said proudly. She went into a natural sway with the baby in her arms against her chest.

Omar didn't know how many more revelations he could take. Before he could think, he said, "You really ought to reconcile with your mother, especially with the baby. This lost time can never be gotten back."

She looked down at her baby and planted a kiss before rubbing her face against the chubby cheeks. "No promises. I'll think about it."

Omar nodded and silently signaled the team to

end the session. He turned to face the young parents. "Thank you again for agreeing to do this. I think that both your mother and Stacy would be proud to see that you've handled your business and without breaking any promises. Give them the gift of a second chance."

"Too late for that."

"What?"

Vince, her partner, took the baby down the hall.

"Too late for second chances. I blew it with Stacy." Valerie looked miserable.

"Stacy was here?" Omar couldn't believe this revelation.

Valerie shook her head. "I told her don't bother showing her face."

"But why? I thought you were friends. What about your mother?"

"Don't you start," she replied, raising her hand to stop his criticisms. "Stacy and I were friends. She outgrew me and never looked back. She told me that she had to talk to me about my mother. It's too late for my mother and a family reunion scene. And then she had the nerve to play on my sympathy by telling me that she has a heart condition."

"She's not kidding."

"Is she in the hospital?" Valerie asked, clearly disbelieving.

"She was and is still recovering." Omar allowed

the information to sink it. "Look, I'm not trying to change anyone's mind. Figured the years would have softened the reaction. You've grown up, she's gotten older."

"And Stacy is now her golden child." Valerie opened the door. "It was a nice interview, Omar. Let's leave it at that."

Chapter 13

"Brenda, I don't have much time." Stacy had to meet Omar by three o'clock for them to head to the airport without rushing.

"I wanted to tell you two things. And one doesn't have anything to do with the other."

Stacy braced herself, expecting some horrific report about Brenda's health. She moved from her position near the doorway and came fully into the room, aiming for the couch.

"I've decided to retire."

"What?" Stacy blinked, trying to rid her head of the confusion.

"I've done what I've set out to do. I've met and surpassed my goals. And you know what?"

Stacy shook her head, still speechless.

"I'm not happy." Brenda opened the bottle of water that was clutched in her hand and took a long drink. "My life, for the most part, sped past me before I could take in anything." She raised her bottle in salutation. "Here's to taking it easy and stopping to smell everything wonderful about life."

"Are you ill?" Stacy blurted. She sheepishly covered her mouth.

"No. But I am sick. Sick of looking after everyone. Sick of the high pressure, high mainte-nance from most of my clients. This heart attack struck me right where I'd notice. Now I'm in the mood to let go and follow my passion."

Stacy worried that maybe Brenda was suffering a breakdown. She had no other passion. As long as she'd known Brenda, she'd worked in the entertain-ment field and managing up-and-coming stars was her skill. Now she wanted to throw it away when she had at least another twenty-odd years of working left in her.

"Are you listening? I'm going to pursue my passion—sculpting." Brenda gave her a twisted smile. "I can see that you don't believe me."

"I do believe you. I don't understand why." She couldn't possibly leave Brenda in this situation.

"Right now I crave solitude. I've lost two young women close to my heart. First my daughter and now you." She sighed. "Sorry, I don't want to be maudlin. No pity parties here." She walked over and placed a hand on Stacy's shoulder.

Stacy saw the unshed tears shimmer. Brenda had lifted her out of the muck in her life. She had been the female force that filled the void left by her mother. She had kept her on the straight and narrow as any father figure would have.

"Have you heard from your daughter?" Stacy questioned. She knew the answer, but went through the motions.

"I did get another letter from her last week. She keeps telling me not to worry, that we will meet soon, that we will talk." This time a tear did fall, tracing a path down her cheek to her chin. "All I keep thinking is that I had a heart attack and she wasn't at my side."

"Would you like to see her?"

"What? What are you saying?" Brenda slowly sank into the chair, sitting on the edge. Her eyes were huge circles full of question and wonder. "You know my daughter?"

Stacy swallowed. She wished that she could run this past someone, but her revelation was about to be a solo act.

"Stacy, do you know Valerie?"

"Yes. I was with her when you discovered me. She had told me about you for several months. We both felt that we were running from pretty horrific things in our life."

Brenda looked down at her hands. "And am I so horrible? Am I such a monster?"

Stacy approached Brenda and sank onto the floor near her. Kneeling there, she looked up into Brenda's sad face. "I know. I kept a stupid promise. But I thought that I could also get you to reconcile."

"Have you talked to her?"

"I tried. She moved and no one knew where she'd gone. I feared for the worst."

"That's my job. That's what I do every night, worrying about my daughter." Brenda laughed bitterly. "You'll have your day soon."

"I did find her." Stacy shuddered at the fact that she had had to talk to Antonio to do it. At least she'd made the worm feel guilty, even if only temporarily.

"And…" Brenda's hand shot out and gripped hers.

Stacy shook her head.

"I don't understand. She wrote that she'd like to meet."

Stacy groaned. How she wished that she was somewhere else, that this conversation didn't need to take place now. "I wrote the letters. I wanted to give you hope."

"And empty promises." Brenda pushed away from her. Her trademark anger snapped from its slumber and blazed down on her. "How dare you? What games are you playing? All this time I thought my daughter was working up her courage to see me. Now to hear that Valerie doesn't give a crap about me, nor you, apparently."

The housekeeper appeared in the doorway, concern on her face. She surveyed them, settling a steely gaze on Stacy. The housekeeper was a little too late; Stacy had already heaped guilt, anger and disgust upon herself.

"I'll leave you now. When I return, I want to take you to your daughter."

"Is that your penitence?" Brenda asked.

Stacy shrugged. Her guilt, her role, her intention didn't matter anymore. "Please think about it." She stood to leave, pausing long enough to see if Brenda would come to a decision.

"I'm tired now. I'll follow up my retirement announcement with a formal letter to you." The housekeeper placed a protective arm around her boss and escorted her from the room.

Stacy took the hint and showed herself out of the house. Once outside she wished that she could breathe a sigh of relief. If Brenda still refused to see Valerie by the time she returned from her visit with Omar, she would have to come up with an alternative plan. Too much time had been wasted, too many lives affected.

She called Omar to let him know that she was on her way. He didn't have a clue about the relationship between Brenda and her. And he certainly didn't know she had sent the letters as her daughter for Brenda's peace of mind. Facing another rejection weighed heavily on her emotions. She couldn't bear to see or feel the sharp reproof that was bound to happen.

Maybe she was a coward. As she retrieved her suitcase to transfer to Omar's car, she relished the thought of escaping for a few days. Omar emerged from his apartment building. The instant she saw his handsome face, smiling with obvious delight at her, her mood lifted. She'd take this little retreat as needed time to set things right with Brenda.

"What a beautiful home," Stacy exclaimed to Omar as he parked in front of his brother's house.

The little garden on the front lawn, the porch and swing, the wind chimes welcomed her. She only hoped that his family would be warm and inviting.

"I'm glad you like it. I think you need a place to regroup." Omar trailed behind her with the suitcases.

"Why would you say that?" If he only knew how close to the truth he'd hit.

"I know how you feel that everyone is pulling at you. I want you to feel safe here."

"Aren't you the romantic?" she teased, loving every minute of his attentive attitude. Already she could feel her shoulders relax.

Before Omar could knock, the door was flung open. Stacy was glad that she stood off to the side as an older woman ran out and launched herself with open arms at Omar. While they greeted each other, a toddler who looked about two years old walked cautiously to the door. The child wrinkled her nose at Stacy, showing her small white teeth.

"You must be Stacy. I'm Haley, Omar's sister-in-law. And this little tyke is Deidre." She scooped the toddler into her arms, raising her to eye level.

"Nice to meet you," Stacy said, returning the same level of enthusism. "And nice to meet you, Deidre." She reached for the little girl's hand, which clutched her outstretched finger.

"Let's get inside. I've got dinner prepared, figuring that you'd be starved. Sheena is going to stop by after work. Laura isn't due in for another couple of hours. Pierce will get her from the airport."

"Do you have room for all of us?" Omar asked.

"Laura will stay with Sheena, you know, considering everything." Haley didn't meet Omar's eyes.

Stacy might not have had the benefit of siblings, but she understood the universal code of verbal and nonverbal cues.

"It's okay, I shared with Stacy that Sheena is separated, on the verge of a divorce." He laid his hand across her shoulder, drawing her into him.

Stacy noticed Haley shift her gaze from Omar to her. There was a quiet understanding that she had been trusted with the family secrets.

"Omar, you're sleeping in Pierce's office."

"What?"

"Stacy is sleeping upstairs." Haley ignored Omar's indignation. "Pierce's orders." She raised her hand in a noncommittal gesture.

"Omar." Stacy tried to get his attention. Her face warmed with embarrassment at his outrage on their behalf. "I prefer it this way." Her admission surprised him into silence. "Put yourself in my place, coming to see your big brother and impressing the family. Let's follow decorum."

Later, Omar sat on the sofa bed in Pierce's office. Though he understood Stacy's point, that didn't mean he liked it. He wanted her at his side. He wanted to feel her body with its delicious curves warm against his body. Instead his brother was playing the father figure again. He punched the pillow with a frustrated thump and grunted his frustration to the empty room.

* * *

Stacy barely tasted the meal that Haley cooked. She couldn't get control of her nerves and handle eating dinner with the entire Masterson family. When Pierce pushed his plate aside, she followed suit.

"Everyone, you must come into the living room for an early viewing of my upcoming project. This is my baby that I've been working on for many long days, but I think it will be worth every ounce of labor," Omar announced, ending any side conversations around the table.

Stacy couldn't help but feel a little left out. Omar hadn't shared his progress on the project with her. Maybe she'd been so caught up with Brenda that she wasn't available to listen to him. His family's excitement rubbed off on her. She threw off any negative feelings and happily followed them into the room.

"Good, we're all seated. Let's get this going," Pierce prompted, earning him a jab in his ribs from Haley.

"Pay no attention to your bully of a brother." Haley glared at Pierce. "Now that you are a famous television host, I want to see everything that you do."

"Everyone, stop talking. You're making me nervous." Omar slipped a disc into the DVD player. "Before I hit the play button, I want to give a brief intro of my upcoming documentary."

"Documentary?" Sheena slapped her knee. "I can't believe my kid brother is going the serious route." She frowned. "It *is* serious and *will* have an impact on people, right?"

"She's our resident militant," Omar explained with a wink to Stacy.

"Hurry up," Stacy urged, joining in the playful ribbing of the family.

"This is a story about homelessness among teenagers." Omar offered Stacy a small smile.

But all Stacy could feel was a cold stab of fear slice through her. She searched his eyes, looking for a sign that he wasn't going to do what she was afraid he would do. Pointedly ignoring her, he turned toward the TV screen and pressed Play.

Haley squeezed her hand and grinned. Stacy only managed a slight twist of her lips. The reason behind her curiosity about the show certainly didn't match the family's.

"This is still a rough draft, but I wanted to give you a sneak peek." Omar took a seat across from Stacy.

The show unfolded with various interviews of current and former homeless teens. Stacy was impressed to see various government officials and administrators from the few teen homeless shelters being interviewed intermittently by a beautiful, dark-haired Latina or Omar.

"As long as this is well rounded, I can deal." A deep frown settled along Pierce's brow.

"What do you mean?" Sheena asked.

"I want to hear from the teens, as well as parents. Some kids have it rough, but then others are just being rebels," Pierce said with a touch of anger.

"Cool it, hon. You'll scare Stacy." Haley nudged Stacy in the side.

Stacy's face warmed under the scrutiny. This family with its strong bonds and love could not know that she was one of those kids. Her insides quivered from the threat of being uncovered. The subjects who responded to Omar's probing questions provided the extreme conditions and experiences of life on the street. She heard the family sighs and sounds of disapproval as many of the kids described their addictions.

Silence settled over the room. Each person focused on the TV screen. Stacy wished that she could get insight into each family member's reaction, pity or indictment. She didn't have the addictions of drugs or alcohol, but nevertheless, she'd spent time with troubled teens. Their misery had been shared, sometimes involuntarily public, but mostly private.

A familiar voice yanked her attention back to the documentary. A voice she'd heard recently. This entire experience had her jumping out of her skin. She stole a glance at Omar and he stared back at her.

"I would consider Stacy Watts my childhood friend. We have since gone our separate ways. But at one time, we shared these mean streets," Valerie said into the camera.

"Well, this is a shock," Pierce declared.

Stacy couldn't tell if this was a good thing. From the way the family had turned to look at her, she didn't perceive the current situation as warm and fuzzy.

"Guess her career got in the way," Valerie added. "Maybe she doesn't want anything to destroy her good-girl image." Valerie looked into the camera. "Not that she wasn't a good girl. Even on the street everyone knew that she was not to be messed with because she was Antonio's girl."

"Who's Antonio?" Pierce blurted.

Haley promptly shushed him.

Stacy looked over at Omar, hoping that he had an escape plan for this heated moment. Pretending that nothing unusual was taking place wasn't possible when all eyes were trained on her. Her shame hung there for public scrutiny, to be examined. Her face burned with the flush of embarrassment.

"Excuse me," Stacy said and ran out of the room toward the front door. All she wanted was fresh air minus the prying eyes.

"Stacy, wait!" Omar shouted.

Stacy stepped onto the porch, gulping in the cool air. She closed her eyes to enjoy the air. She'd heard Omar, but she was hardly going to stand there to discuss anything. With a chance to breathe and collect her thoughts, her anger moved from its low simmer to full-blast.

Omar stepped out on the porch and stuffed his hands in his pockets. He stood against the rail looking out at the traffic. Stacy could reach out and touch him, but didn't. Instead her fingers curled into fists and she folded her arms definitively across her chest.

"Everyone is asking about you in there." Omar kept his back to her.

Stacy turned toward the door half expecting to see faces pressed against the nearby windows. All was quiet.

"I'm guessing that an apology isn't enough." Omar turned and leaned against the rail, his head hung low on his chest.

"You're one hundred percent correct." Stacy struggled to keep her voice level. "I can't understand why you did this to me. I didn't want to be a part of your documentary. But clearly all I am to you is ratings."

"That's not true. How could you think that I would use you?"

"Because everyone has used me. And during my first meeting with your family, you show this ugliness."

"Your life is not ugly. I know that others can learn from it. I've talked to these young girls and many of them are a footstep from a life of drugs, prostitution or jail." Omar threw up his hands. "Sorry, but the situation made me want to do something immediately."

Stacy knew what Omar said sounded right and wholesome. Yet he'd trampled over her private wish, which unsettled her.

"I'm going in to share my regrets with your family that I can't stay. Then I'm leaving. If I can't get a flight out tonight, then I will stay at a hotel." Stacy took a deep breath and headed for the door.

Omar hurried over to her and grabbed her arms. "Please, don't leave. I may have been a jackass for having Valerie in the documentary talking about you, but I promise you that I did it out of love. I love you, Stacy. And I know that my family has a big heart. You're underestimating them."

"Maybe." Stacy pushed him aside and entered

the house. She tried to smile at the family grouped together on the couch. Her mouth merely trembled and the swell of her emotions had her fighting tears. She refused to break down into an emotional mess. She didn't want their pity or their diplomatic words that they understood what she had gone through.

"This was a surprise to you," Pierce said.

Stacy nodded, although it was more of a statement. "I…I will be leaving sooner…" Stacy took a steadying breath. "Thank you for your hospitality."

"Wait a minute. You're leaving?" Haley shot out of the chair and headed over to her. "Please, don't leave. Omar!"

At the sound of Omar's name being called, Stacy pushed away Haley's hand. "I wouldn't make good company at the moment."

"That's okay. Sheena wouldn't make good company, either, but we're stuck with her," Pierce teased, adding a wink to his remarks.

Stacy smiled, appreciating his attempt. "I'll go get my suitcase." She ran from the room before anyone could stop her. Their voices raised in alarm rumbled into one conversation. From their pointed accusations, she gathered that Omar had reentered the room. She continued up the stairs to the guest bedroom.

She'd taken such care in packing for this trip,

all her clothes rolled in tight bundles to go in her suitcase, but now she tossed everything back in and slammed down the top. A light knock on the door made her pause for a second before she resumed her task. She ignored the caller.

"Stacy, it's me," Haley said softly through the door.

"Come in." Stacy kept herself busy, gathering her toiletries. She heard rustling, then the squeak of the mattress. "Are you the peacekeeper?"

Haley chuckled. "I've been called that. And in this case, I'm proud of my title."

"I'm not declaring war on anyone." Well, that was a small lie. Stacy zipped her makeup bag and tossed it into her carry-on luggage.

"Maybe *war* is a strong word. I think we have a tense situation. Yet I don't think that it's the end of the world."

"Of course it's not a big deal. You're a doctor's wife with beautiful children," Stacy huffed, frustrated that no one could really understand.

"Oh, girl, have a seat." Haley sat on the bed and patted the open spot next to her. "Yes, I may have a stable life like a Rockwell painting. But it wasn't always that way. I'd lived a life that I often compared to hell. I worried for my daughter. I worried that I wasn't capable of providing for her as a single parent. And I was at rock bottom when I came to live in this town to start over." Haley patted her hand. "You'll have to work out your issues with Omar. But the family doesn't think any less of you. What little I know of my brother-in-law, I know that he did not mean to hurt you." Haley stood and headed out of the room. "Please reconsider leaving."

Stacy remained in the room, seated on the bed. Haley's invitation was so sincere, working to calm any fears.

"Stacy, sweetheart, hear me out," Omar said from the doorway. He held up his hands in surrender.

"Come in." Stacy moved along the bed, ensuring that his body would not brush against hers if he sat.

"I just got reamed from everyone downstairs," Omar said with a rueful grin. "This was supposed to be a bigger-than-life introduction to the family. I wanted them to be impressed with you, your work ethic, who you've become despite the obstacles." Omar walked over and knelt at her feet. "I wanted them to like you."

"Valerie added to my guilt for escaping that lifestyle. I told Brenda about her daughter. She's beyond angry with me. I'm not feeling too loved right about now."

Omar wedged himself between Stacy's legs

and held his head against her stomach. Stacy looked down at his head, following her heart's request to touch his hair. She stroked his head, following the swirl pattern from the middle, spiraling out toward his hairline.

"That feels good," Omar said, muffled against her clothes. "It's been a while since we've been in each other's arms."

Stacy's hand stilled.

"Don't stop." Omar tightened his hold around her waist. "I may not have had a childhood comparable to yours. I have a strong family support that you didn't have. But what we do have together is our future. We both have careers that have opened paths for us to explore and enjoy. I'm willing to go hand in hand with you down any of those paths. But I also don't think that we have to shut the gate behind us. Our past shaped us. And you have become a beautiful, caring person."

"Valerie doesn't think so."

"Call me sickeningly optimistic, but I don't think anything is impossible. Valerie put up a front to be tough in case you rejected her."

"Why would I reject her? It's because of her that I met Brenda."

Omar settled back on his heels, but still kept his hands at her waist. "Valerie has a little girl. She thought that if you knew she'd gotten pregnant, you'd be disgusted. But more than that, she's afraid of what her mother would think."

Stacy held Omar's face, tilting it up to hers. "A baby?" The tears that she struggled to hold back tumbled down her cheeks. "I can't believe it. Brenda will be so happy when she finds out."

"See, sweetheart, sometimes there is something beautiful that comes out of life's ugliness."

"You're corny." She slid off the bed onto her knees. "But I love you for it."

"You sweet-talker, you."

"You are the beautiful thing in my life." Stacy kissed him, closing her eyes as her lips touched his.

Omar groaned. His arms encircled her body and drew her against his muscled physique. He returned her kiss.

"Um…Uncle Omar, Aunt Sheena sent me to get you," Haley's daughter, Beth, said.

Stacy accepted Omar's hand, helping her up. She corrected the smudges of her lipstick, fluffed her hair and then adjusted her clothes.

"Let's go finish watching that documentary, sweetheart." Holding Omar's hand, Stacy followed him down the stairs.

The family cheered as the couple descended. Their raucous ovation welcomed her. She gladly embraced their effusive outpouring. She suspected that she'd need Omar and their love and compassion as she worked through her nightmares. She still had to create a happy ending between Brenda and her daughter. With Omar's firm backing, she had a resurgence of confidence that Brenda had not lost her daughter and Valerie had not lost her mother.

"I don't care who's watching." Omar spun her into his arms. Like a prince awakening her from a deep slumber, he lowered his head and melded their lips together.

When Stacy could suck in some air, she grabbed Omar's chin. "You're all mine. I love you for it." She kissed him, vaguely aware of the roar that ascended.

"I love you," Omar whispered into her ear.

"And I love and want you," Stacy responded.

Wanted: Good Christian woman

ESSENCE BESTSELLING AUTHOR

Jacquelin Thomas

The Pastor's Woman

New preacher Wade Kendrick wants a reserved, traditional
woman for a wife—but he only has eyes for Pearl Lockhart,
aka Ms. Wrong. Pearl aspires to gospel stardom and doesn't
fit into the preacher's world. But their sexual chemistry
downright sizzles. What's a sister to do?

THE LOCKHARTS
THREE WEDDINGS AND A REUNION
FOR FOUR SASSY SISTERS, ROMANCE CHANGES EVERYTHING!

Available the first week of September wherever books are sold.

KIMANI™
ROMANCE

Grown and sultry...

CANDICE POARCH

As a girl, Jasmine wanted Drake desperately, but
Drake considered his best friend's baby sister
completely off-limits. Now Jasmine is all grown up,
and goes to work for Drake, and he's stunned by the
explosive desire he feels for her. Even though she still
has way too much attitude, Drake finds himself
unable to resist the sassy, sexy beauty....

*Available the first week of September
wherever books are sold.*

He was the first man to touch her soul...

SOUL Caress

Favorite author

KIM SHAW

When privileged Kennedy Daniels loses her sight, hospital orderly Malik Crawford helps heal her wounds and awaken her desire. But they come from different worlds, so unless Kennedy's willing to defy her prominent family, a future between them is impossible.

Available the first week of September wherever books are sold.

KIMANI™
ROMANCE